HEARTS IN EXILE

Two teachers are evacuated from Coventry to the Welsh countryside, where they struggle with wartime hardship as they help their pupils adjust to a different way of life. Will love follow them there? Vivacious Tansy sees marriage as a way to escape her impoverished background, while shy Dinah just wants to find someone to love. She falls for handsome Emlyn, but the young Welshman is equally reserved. How will they ever get together?

CATRIONA McCUAIG

HEARTS IN EXILE

Complete and Unabridged

LINFORD
Leicester

First published in Great Britain in 2011

First Linford Edition
published 2012

British Library CIP Data

McCuaig, Catriona.
　Hearts in exile.- -(Linford romance library)
　1. Love stories.
　2. Large type books.
　I. Title II. Series
　813.6–dc23

　ISBN 978–1–4448–1217–6

Published by
F. A. Thorpe (Publishing)
Anstey, Leicestershire

Set by Words & Graphics Ltd.
Anstey, Leicestershire
Printed and bound in Great Britain by
T. J. International Ltd., Padstow, Cornwall

1

Dinah moved wearily in her seat as the train sped onward into the night. Would this miserable journey never end? All around her children were slumped in their seats, stirring occasionally, or muttering in their sleep. Poor little devils! Wasn't it bad enough that there was a war on, without children being torn away from everything they knew and loved and sent into exile?

Come to that, she wasn't too happy herself. She had never been far from Coventry before, not unless you counted the one seaside holiday they'd managed when she was a child. It had been a struggle for her widowed mother to bring up two children — Dinah and her younger sister, Joyce — after their father died. Joe Blake had served in the Great War and been invalided out after suffering from a gas attack. He had never recovered his health, and although he and his Alice had tried to make the best of things and had gone on to have two children, he had never been able to work again. He had died when Dinah was barely three, just another victim of the 'war to end all wars'.

Now, twenty years on, here they were, embroiled in another conflict. 'It makes me thankful I've only got daughters,' Alice Blake had said, when they heard the Prime Minister making the announcement on the wireless.

'Why's that, Mum?' Joyce was staring at herself in a hand mirror, pulling up a tuft of hair and winding it round her fingers. 'Do you think I'd better get a perm next time? I hate it when my hair goes all flat like this.'

'Isn't it obvious? Men have to go to war and get themselves killed. At least you two can stay home with me, where you'll be safe . . . and exactly where are you going to get the money for a perm? They don't come cheap, you know!'

'Oh, Mum!'

'Don't you 'oh, Mum,' me, Joyce Blake! The next thing I know you'll be asking to borrow from me, and that's the last I'll see of my hard-earned cash! I don't slave away in that shop for the fun of it, you know.'

Neither girl was listening. They had heard it all before. But now, on the train, Dinah remembered what her mother had said. She'd been wrong, of course. Women as well as men, were in this one up to their necks. They'd all had to register and were likely to be called up into the services, unless they were directed into factory work.

'You won't have to go, Dinah, you being a school teacher,' Alice had told her. 'As for you, Joyce Blake, you'd better find yourself a local job, for I won't have you joining the WAAFs or the like.'

'No fear!' Joyce grumbled. 'I don't fancy the uniforms. All those bulky pockets. I'm going to sign on as a clippie on the buses, that's what.'

'They'll have you wearing trousers,

like the men,' Alice warned, but Joyce only laughed. 'Worse things happen at sea, Mum!'

Dinah admired her sister's cheeky attitude. She could just see her working as a bus conductress, issuing tickets and exchanging banter with the passengers. She longed to be more like Joyce, always bubbling over with fun, and giving as good as she got in any encounter. But it was no good wishing, as Alice was fond of saying, for Dinah had been born shy.

That was one reason why she'd gone in for teaching. Standing in front of a class of youngsters, knowing that she was doing a worthwhile job, gave her great satisfaction. She didn't feel shy there, and she didn't have to compete with prettier, more outgoing girls.

Not that Mum and Joyce didn't conspire to involve her in a social life. 'You need taking out of yourself, my girl,' Mum would say, each time Joyce went to a 'hop' and Dinah refused to go along with her. But Dinah was happy as she was and refused to be persuaded. The one time she had given in and taken part, it was worse than she'd feared. Nobody asked her to dance and she'd had to sit on the sidelines, watching gloomily as Joyce jitterbugged happily with one chap after another.

'Are you a wallflower?' That had been the question posed by the agony aunt in her mother's magazine the previous week. Dinah had to admit that she was. Trying to follow the advice given by the expert, she'd pasted a smile on her face, and tried to 'talk animatedly' with her neighbour. Finally, when even the girl with acne and rabbity teeth was swept onto the floor by an equally spotty youth, she'd given up the struggle, taking refuge in the ladies' cloakroom.

Joyce had followed her in. 'Having a good time, are you?'

'No, I'm not.'

'Oh, don't be such an idiot, Dinah! Look, come back in and I'll dance with you. All right?'

'No, it's not all right. You can stay if

5

you like, but I'm going home.'

'Oh, be like that, then!'

Alice, of course, was sympathetic. But then, what are mothers for? 'Never mind, love,' she'd said gently. 'I'll make you a nice cup of tea. You don't have to go again if you don't want to.'

'But what's wrong with me, Mum?' Dinah had wailed. 'Why can't I be more like Joyce?'

'Now, now. None of that! We're all different, love. Perhaps you could sign up for an evening class instead. Learn dressmaking, or first aid.'

'What on earth for?'

'Why, to meet somebody nice, of course. You want to get married some day, don't you? Although come to think of it, there might not be many eligible young men going there to make themselves a nice summer frock. Perhaps you'd better take up carpentry instead!'

Alice was joking, of course. Always one to look for the positive in any situation, she spoke cheerfully when Dinah had arrived home from school with the news that their small school was being evacuated to Wales.

'Well, that will make a change, won't it, love! All that lovely Welsh countryside. I wouldn't mind coming with you myself.'

'I thought it was all coal mines and that.'

'Nonsense! I've seen pictures. I don't know what it will be like where you're going, but I'm sure you'll enjoy being in new surroundings. You'll have to write and tell me all about it.'

'Of course I'll write, Mum. If they keep us there for very long, perhaps you could come for a bit of a holiday. I could show you the sights.'

'You can count me out,' Joyce muttered. 'I bet there won't be a decent dance hall within miles.'

'And a good thing too, my girl!' Alice told her, frowning. 'You spend a great deal too much time in those places for my liking. Those shoes of yours have to go to the cobbler's again. All that bopping and hopping is too hard on them.'

Joyce pouted. 'I pay my way, don't I?

You get most of my wage packet for my board and lodging, and anything left over is mine to spend as I like — you said.'

'All right, all right! Let's leave it at that, shall we?'

Dinah grinned. She would miss all this when she left home. Mum veering between worrying about her daughters on one hand, and dispensing cheerful words of wisdom to all and sundry on the other. Then there was her feisty younger sister, always determined to extract the best from life. There might be a war on, but Joyce Blake was going to enjoy herself when she could in spite of it.

As for Dinah, she had always been the responsible elder sister — the careful one. Look before you leap, that was her motto. Well, she hadn't had a chance to consider her options before being pitched headlong into this move to another country; the war had seen to that. At least she couldn't be expected to attend dances, where her embarrassing wallflower status would

8

be maintained. As far as she knew, there would be no dancing in Bryncollen, where the chapels reigned supreme.

Once again the train jerked to a halt. Billy Watson sat up, rubbing his eyes. 'Are we there yet, Miss?'

'I don't think so, Billy. Go back to sleep now, there's a good boy. It will make the time go faster.'

'That's what my mum always says on Christmas Eve, Miss.'

'And I'm sure she's right.'

'I can't wait to go to the beach, Miss. I want to built a sandcastle, like those boys did in the book you read us.'

Dinah sighed. She was aware that some well-meaning parents had tried to soften the blow of their impending separation by explaining to the children that they were going on a lovely holiday. One little girl had even brought a bucket and spade to school on the day of their departure, and had wept inconsolably when she was made to leave it behind.

There was no beach where they were

going, but possibly Wales would provide other diversions. With a jerk, the train started up again. Dinah leaned forward and rubbed her aching back.

★　★　★

'Thomas Fry! If I see you flinging that yo-yo about just once more, I'll confiscate it, and you won't get it back until we come back to Coventry, if at all!' Dora Ramsey bellowed across the train coach.

'Aw Miss! It's not fair! You're letting them girls play, so why can't I?'

'Those girls are playing cat's cradle,' Dora countered. 'They can't do much harm with a few bits of string. As for that yo-yo, you could have someone's eye out if you're not careful. It's not meant to be played with in such a confined space. Sit down and read your comic.'

'I already looked at it twice, Miss.'

'Then look at it again.'

The boy subsided, muttering.

She could understand his frustration. Seated in the adjoining compartment with a number of older pupils, Dora wondered how Dinah Blake was coping with the little ones. The corridor train on which they'd travelled earlier in the day had at least provided access to the lavatories, cramped and grubby though they were. In hindsight she wondered now if they should have brought a potty with them, but how could they have known that this small local train would have no facilities? Just as well, perhaps, for she couldn't see any child performing in front of an audience. No, if there were any wet knickers at least they were prepared for that eventuality, with three clean pairs hidden in her huge carpet bag.

As Deputy Head, Dora was responsible for such matters. In fact, since Mr Pepper had remained behind, she was, in effect, Acting Head. As a married woman she had never expected to reach such dizzy heights. Prior to her marriage to Jim Ramsey she had

11

enjoyed a brief teaching career at Soper Street School, but she had been compelled to resign following the wedding, back in 1924.

In those days women who entered professions such as teaching and nursing were not permitted to work at them after marriage because of the long hours involved. How could they be expected to give their all to the job, while trying to look after a husband and children at the same time? Housework alone was demanding enough when there were few labour-saving devices available.

Sadly, the longed-for children failed to appear, and Dora soon found her role as a housewife to be unrewarding. Putting their tiny flat to rights was the work of an hour or less, and then the rest of the day stretched before her, in all its boredom. Without saying a word to Jim she had gone down to the school to ask for her job back.

'But can't you make an exception?' she had asked the then-headmaster, Mr

Phelps. 'I don't have children, and I'm a good teacher. When I left two years ago you told me I'd be missed.'

'I'm sorry, Mrs Ramsey,' he'd told her. 'The rules are set down very clearly by the Board. Besides, what would your husband say if you had your way? I don't think he'd be any too pleased.'

And of course Mr Phelps was right. When Dora had confessed what she had done, Jim Ramsey blew up like a volcano. 'What would people think if I sent my wife out to work? They'd say I couldn't afford to keep her! No man wants that! And before you even think of going out and getting work as a shop assistant, the same thing applies. When I married you I vowed to keep you in comfort, and so I have. I've kept my part of the bargain, and you'll keep yours, or you'll feel the back of my hand!'

Dora knew it was all talk. Jim had never lifted a finger to her, but this bravado had been some indication of how strongly he felt. Sadly, she told herself to make the best of what she had, and be thankful.

It was strange, then, that the war had made all the difference. Dora had been surprised to receive a note from the current Head, Robert Pepper, asking her to call at Soper Street after classes were over for the day. Puzzled, she'd put on her Sunday hat and walked to the school, her heart thumping as she went.

'Ah, Miss Pusey. How nice to see you ... Mrs Ramsey, I should say.' Mr Pepper had been one of the senior masters when Dora had been there as a young teacher, so she knew the man slightly. He was grey-haired now, and slightly stooped.

'You wanted to see me, Mr Pepper?'

'Ah, yes. There's a war on, you see.'

Surely the man hadn't brought her all the way down here to tell her that? Ever since war had been declared six months earlier, there hadn't been a man, woman or child in England who hadn't been aware of that.

'As a result, we've lost three of our masters. That is to say, two have joined up, and the third expects to be called up at any moment. To cut a long story short, you're needed here, Mrs Ramsey. Would you be willing to come back to us? We're not likely to find any suitable male teachers who are free to come, unless it's some old boy who comes creaking back out of retirement.'

Dora's heart had leapt. Of course she would! 'I'd have to speak to my husband,' she said. 'He's a bit old-fashioned, I'm afraid.'

'Doesn't like the idea of his wife going out to work, I suppose. I'm afraid that's likely to happen in any case, the way things are going,' Mr Pepper mused. 'One of these days you could find yourself in one of the women's services, posted far from Coventry. I suggest you remind Mr Ramsey of that. I'm sure he'd prefer you to be working here, within a stone's throw of home, hmm?'

Dora nodded. Too excited to go

directly home, she had taken a detour through a pretty park, where she sank down on an empty bench. To teach again! She couldn't believe her luck. Jim simply must be persuaded. Yes, she had been away from the job for sixteen years, but surely teaching methods could not have changed that much? She could exchange news with the rest of the staff, and she would soon catch up.

She had jumped to her feet, planning to call at the Home & Colonial on the way home, to buy ingredients for Jim's favourite tea. Before springing any unwelcome news on him, it was always best to soften him up first.

As it happened, Jim had news of his own, news which quite took the wind out of her sails.

'Sit down, love. I've something you need to hear.'

'Oh? What's that, then?'

He cleared his throat. 'Um . . . I've . . . well, here's the thing,' he stumbled awkwardly. 'I've joined up.'

'You've done what?'

'I've joined the Army. I've been to a recruiting office and signed on. Passed the medical and all,' he'd said, almost proudly.

'But why would you do such a thing, Jim? I mean, you're almost forty! Surely you're too old?'

He'd grinned. 'I'm fit, aren't I? All I had to do was shave a few years off my age, and nobody the wiser.'

'But your birth certificate . . . '

'Nobody asked for it and why should they?' he'd told her. 'They can see I'm no fifteen-year-old.'

'And you didn't think of discussing this with me first?'

'Don't be cross, love. Try to understand. I missed the last show by a whisker and I've always regretted it. Now's my big chance, see?'

'Your chance to get killed, you mean!'

'Don't be like that, Dora.'

'Then just see how you like this! I've been invited to go back to Soper Street, and I've jumped at the chance,' she'd retorted.

'What? I don't think so. I'm not having that! I want you here, waiting for me when I come home on leave.'

'And so I shall be. The school is only ten minutes' walk from home. Fifteen if I go the long way round past the shops.' Dora had been determined not to back down now.

They had argued long into the night, and at last Jim Ramsey had to concede that this war had indeed made a difference in people's lives, as his wife put it.

Within weeks he had gone away to basic training, and Dora had returned to the school.

Now the wheel of fortune had made yet another turn, and now here she was, in charge of a large portion of that school as they went into exile into the countryside, far from home and hearth, to another country even.

'But won't you be coming with us, Mr Pepper?' she'd blurted, when news of the pending evacuation had been announced. 'What will you do, if the

18

school is empty?'

'I was due for retirement a year ago, so I'd be leaving in any case if the war hadn't come. I shall join the Home Guard, Mrs Ramsey, and prepare to fight the Hun on British soil if the invasion comes, God forbid.'

As she recalled those stirring words the train slowed, and this time it seemed as if they had reached the end of their journey at last.

Thomas Fry let the window down with a crash, and stuck his head out as the train steamed into the station. 'We're here, Miss, we're here!'

'Don't you dare open that door until I say the word!' Dora roared, standing up to reach for her suitcase. A fine thing it would be if they'd escaped the war, only to have some child injured even before they reached their new billets.

As Acting Headmistress, she prepared to go into action.

2

Dinah took a deep breath as she climbed the hill overlooking the town, thankful to find her stress ebbing away. She stopped for a moment to enjoy the view. Bryncollen was a very pretty place. She really must bring her class up here for a walk, where they could gather specimens for the nature table she intended to set up.

She wondered how the children were settling in. She'd planned to call in at each one at their foster homes, if that was the right name for their temporary refuge from the perils of war — but when the three teachers had come together that morning, Mrs Ramsey had shaken her head.

'We must give them time to get used to the idea of being away from home, dear. I expect that the women who have taken them in will be more than capable of providing the comfort they need.'

'But some of them were crying when we got here last night.'

'Of course they were, dear. I felt like having a little weep myself. We were all exhausted and hungry after the long journey. I'm sure they nodded off as soon as they were tucked into bed, and they'll feel fighting fit after a good night's sleep.'

'I don't know about that. First they're dragged away from their parents, with labels attached to them, as if they're parcels to be sent goodness knows where, then they have to line up on the platform here waiting to be claimed by strangers, speaking a strange language. They must feel as if they've landed on the moon!'

'And what was the alternative, Miss Blake? Leave them in Coventry when there's a war on? At least they'll be safe here.'

'Pooh!' Tansy Smith interrupted. 'Coventry's safe enough. There might

21

be some sense in taking children out of London, but nothing's going to happen to the Midlands. I'll bet you anything they'll be calling us back in no time.'

'We can only hope,' Dora said. 'Meanwhile I have a meeting with the headmaster today — the Meistr, as my landlady calls him. Mr Evans to us. We have to discuss accommodation for our classes. So off you go and enjoy yourselves.'

'But the children . . . ' Dinah persisted.

'You'll see them on Monday morning, Miss Blake. Now, you've got the whole weekend to get to know Bryncollen, so off you go, I suggest you make the most of it.'

So here Dinah was, relishing the solitude. Coming to a halt beside a sturdy fence, she noticed a wooded area in the distance that looked inviting. There was a stile set in the fence and almost without thinking she hopped over it and made her way across the rough ground.

She had just reached the trees when a volley of Welsh reached her ears. At least, she supposed it was Welsh! It might as well have been Greek, for all she knew.

She stopped, bewildered. Coming towards her was a man dressed in rough tweeds, some sort of gamekeeper, perhaps. Was he about to warn her about a roving bull, or something equally dangerous?

He reached her, his eyes blazing. 'Ble wyt ti'n mynd?'

'I don't speak Welsh,' she faltered.

He doffed his cap, revealing curly black hair. He was actually quite good looking.

'I asked you where you think you are going, Miss.'

'Er, just to this wood.' She had no idea how to address him.

'Oh, one of those nutters, are you?'

'I beg your pardon!'

'Strangers who come picking our nuts! Don't you know there's a war on? Or don't they have food rationing in England?'

'Of course we do.'

'Then you should know that we sell those nuts in the market. This isn't the first time I've had to put trespassers off the land. There's an orchard on the other side, with apples and pears. I've caught people stealing those, as well. Last week I caught two men filling bushel baskets with the fruit. It's getting to the point where we're thinking of setting the dogs on people who have no business here.'

'I'm sorry,' Dinah muttered. 'I didn't know I was trespassing, and I'm not a thief.' She thought guiltily that if she had come across a hazel tree she might well have helped herself to a handful of nuts, but he had stopped her in the nick of time. 'I was just exploring the district. We only arrived in Bryn Colin last night.'

'It's pronounced collen, see?' he said, making a throat-clearing sound. 'It means hazel. Lots of hazel trees there must have been in these parts, years ago.'

'Oh.' Dinah saw to her relief that he had wiped the scowl off his face.

'You're one of those evacuees, then, are you?' he asked. 'I heard you were all coming.'

'Yes, I'm a teacher.'

'Then you'll have to teach the little devils not to scrump our apples, won't you? If they're anything like our local boys they'll need telling more than once! Come now, and I'll escort you off the property.'

Dinah had no choice but to follow him, and soon she was standing on the road once more, feeling silly. He doffed his cap to her and strode off, whistling. She was almost at the bottom of the hill when she met Tansy.

'Hello, Di! Out for a walk, are we?'

Of all the stupid questions, Dinah thought. She was rather in awe of Tansy Smith, who was older and much more glamorous than herself. At any other time she would have countered with a meek 'yes', but now she was rattled after her encounter with that gamekeeper person.

'I wouldn't keep going up that way,' she said. 'I just had a run-in with a man up there, who told me I was trespassing.'

'Oh, yes? Good looking, was he?'

'I didn't notice.'

Tansy grinned. 'Too scared to size up the talent? I'll have to take you in hand, my girl! Anyway, I'm glad I met you. I'm looking for a café, if there is a such a thing in this place. I'm desperate for a cup of tea.'

'Didn't your landlady give you breakfast?'

'If you can call it that. One measly cuppa and two bits of toast, miserable old crow. She's got my ration book now, so here's hoping she'll do better next week, or I'll have something to say about it. Now, are you coming with me, or not?'

'I think I'll go back to the house. I promised Mum I'd write as soon as I could, to let her know we arrived safely.' Dinah ignored the other girl's rolling eyes. She knew that Mum would be anxious, so what was wrong with setting her mind at ease?

Her own landlady, one Gwladys Richards, was shaking out a mat just outside
the front door when Dinah arrived. She
smiled broadly and greeted her with a
hearty, 'Here you are, back already!
Meet anybody on your walk, did you?'

'I'm afraid I got into trouble with a
man I met near the wood up the hill
there. I was only exploring, but as it
turns out I was apparently trespassing
on private property, a place with
orchards and a nutwood.'

'Oh, aye? Old Williams, was it?'

'Who?'

'Brian Williams. English, really, not
one of us. Owns the estate, he does, as
well as practically everything else round
here. He's bound to be a bit crotchety-
like, for he has three sons, and every
one of them has just joined the services.
They say his poor wife is nearly
demented with it all, but we've all got
to do our bit, haven't we?'

'This was a younger man. One of the

sons, perhaps? Quite good looking, with black curly hair.'

'Oh, so you've met our Emo, have you? That's Emlyn Rees, my sister's son. You'll be seeing a lot of him, for he's hardly ever off the doorstep. He comes over to give my Twm a hand, see.'

Dinah already knew that Thomas Richards — Twm, for short — repaired furniture in his workshop at the end of the garden. Injured in a mine cave-in years earlier, he'd carved out this new career to support his family.

'I suppose he'll have to manage on his own when Emlyn goes into the Army, then,' she said.

'What? Oh, no. Our Emo won't be joining up, much as he wants to. It's his chest, see? They found a spot on the lung two or three years ago and he spent a bit of time in the sanitorium. They caught it in time, they say, but there's no Army for him. Mr Williams gave him that job when the other chap was called up, and glad to get it, he was.

Outdoors work is good for him, see? That's what the doctor told Bron . . . that's my sister. She wants to meet you, but she's too busy for the moment, with those three little boys she's had billeted on her.'

Dinah felt a frisson of excitement. So the dark-eyed Welshman was practically a son of the house, and she'd be getting to know him better as time went by. For a few moments she indulged in a little fantasy in which she was exploring Bryncollen, with Emlyn Rees at her side. He might even teach her a few words of Welsh, that musical tongue which was the language of princes and bards.

Then she told herself to forget any nonsense like that. Tansy Smith was sure to set her cap at him, and that would be the end of that. It would be a case of Joyce Blake all over again. Joyce always envied what her sister had, and she had never failed to take what she wanted.

★ ★ ★

'You'll want to go to All Saints this morning, I suppose,' Gwladys Richards murmured, as she placed a plate of sizzling bacon and eggs in her husband's place. One egg or two, Miss Blake?'

'One, please.' Dinah was not used to seeing two eggs on the same plate, with everything being rationed so stringently, but things seemed to be different in the country, where people kept their own laying hens.

There's silly I am,' Gwladys went on. 'Of course you want to go to church, you being a teacher in a Church of England school. All I meant was, you'd be very welcome to come to chapel with us, if it suited.'

'The poor girl wouldn't understand a word the minister said,' Twm Richards pointed out.

'Hellfire and brimstone is the same in any language,' his wife retorted. 'It's Maldwyn Evans preaching this morning, and you know well what he's like. Calling sinners by name, and pointing the finger at the rest of us, trying to

30

catch us out if we've done something he hasn't heard about.'

Twm grunted. Dinah felt sorry that she couldn't be present to witness the goings-on. It all sounded like good theatre — just so long as you were an innocent bystander.

'I understand that Mr Evans is also the headmaster at the school?'

Mrs Richards laughed. 'Na, na, cariad. Not at all. This is a different Evans, no relation. Evans the Milk, see?'

Dinah nodded, not understanding at all. 'Perhaps I will come with you some other time, but Mrs Ramsey wants us at All Saints this morning, something about looking at the Sunday School rooms.'

'That's right, cariad; you must do as your headmistress tells you, and you won't go far wrong. D'you want another piece of fried bread, Twm?'

'Aye, and another rasher to put on top of it.' The pair lapsed into Welsh then, and Dinah excused herself to get ready for church.

When Matins was over, made comfortable by the prayers and hymns they were used to at home, the three teachers shook hands with the rector and went outside.

'After consulting me, Mr Evans has decided that it would be best if we hold classes for the Soper Street children here in the parish hall,' Dora explained. 'I thought we should have a look at the Sunday School classrooms to see if they'll suit our purpose.'

'Well, this is a fine welcome, I must say!' Tansy looked as if she was ready to do battle with all comers.

'Just let me explain, Miss Smith. Apart from the danger of overcrowding, we can hardly put our pupils in among the local children.'

'I don't see why not!'

'Well, I do. I'm told that most of the lessons at Bryncollen School are held in Welsh. Our lot would be floundering in no time. It might be different if our children were meant to take up permanent residence in Carmarthen-shire, then they'd have to learn Welsh, but we'll be returning home to Coventry soon, please God!'

Tansy was still prepared to argue. 'My cousin's school was evacuated to a place in Gloucestershire. They rear-ranged the hours so that her class went to school in the mornings, and the local kiddies afternoons.'

'That was one suggestion made by Mr Evans, but I turned it down. First of all, it would have meant our getting up at six o'clock, to be at the blackboard by seven. Or, if we took the afternoon shift, it would have meant the little ones walking back to their billets in the dark, once winter sets in, and possibly getting themselves lost in unfamiliar country. Setting up in the church hall seemed like the lesser of the two evils.'

'But what are the facilities like?'

'That's what we're about to find out, as soon as the rector is free to show us. There won't be desks, of course, but I'm informed that there are perfectly good tables and chairs, and surely they can find us a blackboard from somewhere,' Dora told them firmly. 'As for school supplies, a crate will be coming on the next train, bringing all our books and such from Soper Street.'

'It sounds as if you've got it all worked out,' was Tansy's grudging response to this.

Dinah began to feel better. There was to be no intrusion into the local school, where their appearance might be resented. She would be teaching her own little band of children, and in return her presence would surely be of some comfort to the youngsters themselves. They might have left their mothers behind, but at least they had a familiar face in their own Miss Blake.

She was sad that not all the kiddies had come with them. Some parents had sent their little ones to grandparents or friends in the country, where they would remain for the duration. Others, like Bobby Butcher's mother, had vowed to keep their children close at hand.

'As I was saying to our Sid,' Mrs Butcher had told Dinah, 'our three are better off here, where I can keep an eye on them. Lot of nonsense this, splitting up families. Heaven knows what it may lead to. Juvenile delinquency, I shouldn't wonder! And if that man Hitler does get this far, which I seriously doubt, then we'll all go together. I don't want to die knowing I've left my children orphaned.'

The few remaining children scarcely warranted keeping the school open, so the Soper Street pupils were divided up between other schools in the district. Dinah had given these children her address, urging them to keep in touch by post, but she did not expect to hear from any of them. Most were too young to write a coherent letter without adult help, and there was a war on. Most parents were working harder than ever before, and had little time to spare for tasks that could well be ignored.

'Wake up, dreamy! Didn't you hear what I said?'

Dinah came to with a start, suddenly aware of her surroundings. 'Er, did you say something, Tansy?'

A sly look came over the other girl's face. 'I said, I've met your friend!'

'What friend?' Dinah asked, puzzled. 'Has somebody here come from Coventry, too?'

'No, silly, that Mr Rees. Quite something, isn't he?' Tansy grinned.

'How did you manage that?'

Tansy laughed. 'I did the same thing as you, didn't I? I climbed over the stile and walked towards the wood. Sure enough, up he popped, shouting at me as if I was about to run off with the family silver.'

'Oh, yes?' Dinah said trying to sound casual.

'Don't pretend you aren't interested, Dinah Blake! As it happens, he's asked me out. We're going walking this afternoon. He says he wants to show me the district, so I won't run the risk

36

of trespassing again.'

'That's nice for you,' Dinah managed to say.'

'Oh, well, he's all right to be going on with, I suppose. Mind you, the one I really want is that Williams chap, the one with the red hair.'

'I don't think I know who you mean.'

'Come on, girl; you must have noticed those people in the Williams family pew. An older couple, and their three sons. I fancied the one sitting on the end, next to the aisle.'

Well, of course Dinah had noticed the family. Who could have missed them, especially since the father had got up to read the first lesson? She had assumed that the three younger men, all smartly dressed, although not yet in uniform, were the sons of the family. She must ask her landlady more about them. Very likely they would all become officers, being sons of the landed gentry; perhaps they had already signed on and were awaiting orders. If they were already serving, it seemed unlikely that they'd all be given leave at once.

In any event, Tansy would have to move fast if she intended to get her hooks into the red-headed one. And just how did she propose to wangle an introduction? She could hardly march up to the front door of the house and demand to meet him. Dinah chuckled quietly to herself, imagining the door being opened by a uniformed maid, directing the unwelcome visitor to the back door.

Perhaps she intended to use Emlyn Rees as a way to gain admission. Dinah could imagine her simpering, begging to be shown the house and grounds. She would wait until they came within sight of the house itself, then she would find some excuse to get inside. She would feel faint and need to be given a glass of water. Then she would be too weak to go on and would have to find a place to lie down. Dinah knew Tansy of old and she wouldn't put anything past her.

These wild thoughts were interrupted

by the appearance of a silver-haired man, who came striding across the graveyard, a welcoming smile on his face. Tansy gave her a nudge.

'He must have been a bit of all right when he was younger!'

Dinah hung her head for shame. 'For goodness sake keep your voice down — he'll hear you!'

Tansy smirked. 'I can't get over this place, Di! All these good-looking chaps! Plenty to choose from, I'd say, wouldn't you?'

'Shush!' Dinah hissed, as she caught sight of a frown directed at them by their headmistress.

3

Dinah glared at herself in the mirror. A pale copy of herself stared back. A plain Jane, if ever there was one, she decided. She hoped that the tiny mirror on the wall above the chest of drawers was what her mother would call 'an unkind glass', but it was hard to tell. The mirror was too far from the window, and the light cast by the one low wattage bulb was no help.

She had a pretty, tip-tilted nose, and full lips. Her eyes were best described as grey, although sometimes they seemed to be blue, or even green, depending on the colour of the clothes she was wearing. All those things should have added up to make her a lovely young woman, but she felt that somehow prettiness had passed her by.

She bunched up her dark hair in one hand, wondering if she ought to get it cut. She'd been growing it with the intention of wearing it in a victory roll, like Mrs Ramsey, whom she greatly admired, but it was at that in-between stage where it only looked untidy.

'What I need is a bit of colour,' she muttered, turning back to the bed, where she had been laying out her clothes, ready for Monday morning. The same old jumper and skirt, because she didn't have the clothing coupons to purchase anything new. Joyce had pinched the few she'd been saving, saucily pretending to apologise, 'only I simply must have a new dance frock, Di. You don't know what it's like, wearing a horrid uniform all day on the buses,' she'd said.

Half the trouble was her pale skin, Dinah decided. Her only lipstick was worn down to a stub, and that was the only cosmetic she owned. She pinched one cheek, noting that the pink blush that resulted was quite becoming; if only briefly. What she needed was a bit of rouge. She scowled at her reflection.

'Don't be so wet, Dinah Blake,' she whispered. 'There's no point feeling sorry for yourself. Get up and do something about it.' She would go and call on Tansy, and ask for some tips on make-up. The other girl also had a large collection of chiffon scarves. Perhaps she would lend her one. A red one would go a long way towards livening up Dinah's old brown jumper.

'Who are you?' asked Tansy's land-lady, in charming greeting. Mari Matthews was a plump woman, her head festooned with steel curlers. She glared at poor Dinah as if she meant to slam the door in her face.

'I'm Dinah Blake. I'd like to speak to Miss Smith, please.'

'Well, you can't, see? She isn't here, the hussy!'

'I beg your pardon?' By the woman's tone Dinah gathered that Tansy wasn't held in high favour, although what she could have done to alienate this woman in so short a time, she couldn't imagine. So far they'd only spent a few nights under the same roof.

'She paints her face. You should have seen her going out just now, with cascara on her eyelashes and her lips as red as blood — and on the Sabbath day, too!'

Dinah struggled to hide a smile. She doubted if even Tansy would put cascara, a powerful laxative, on her face. The woman must mean mascara. 'Did she say when she'd be back?'

'She did not, and if she hadn't been foisted on me by that billeting woman, I wouldn't let her over the doorstep again, I can tell you.'

'I think you'll find that Tansy is quite a nice person, when you get to know her,' Dinah said, feeling that she should stand up for her colleague.

'Humph!'

'Well, I'd better be going, then. Will you tell her I called?'

The woman took a step backwards, slamming the door as she did so. Dinah found herself looking at peeling paint. She felt a sudden urge to open the

43

letter box and shout but common sense prevailed in time. The evacuees from Soper Street might be here for a long time, and there was no point in alienating the natives from the word go!

She strolled on towards the centre of Bryncollen, where the shops were. Nothing would be open, of course, this being Sunday, but she might as well get her bearings now.

'Hello! What are you doing here?'

Engrossed in a display of cardigans in a draper's shop window, Dinah hadn't heard Tansy coming up behind her.

'I could ask you the same question! Weren't you supposed to be meeting Emlyn Rees? Didn't he turn up?'

Tansy rolled her eyes. 'He turned up all right, but his idea of a hot date was to take me across a muddy field, to show me a local beauty spot.'

'What's wrong with that?'

'Take a look at my shoes, Di,' Tansy said pointing despondently.

Dinah looked. Tansy was wearing a pair of red leather court shoes with three-inch heels. They were beautiful, but hardly suitable for a country walk. 'I see what you mean.'

'Well, that's more than he did. 'Don't you have any wellies?' he said, like I'm a land girl or something. I ask you!'

Looking her colleague up and down, Dinah could see why Mrs Matthews was scandalised. Tansy was obviously dressed to kill, with a skirt that was rather too short and a jumper that was a fraction too tight. Her blonde hair, which on school days was arranged in plaits on top of her head, was now flowing loose to almost cover one eye, like the photos of film star Veronica Lake. The ensemble would not have been out of place in a larger town, but here in the Welsh hills it was a bit much.

Dinah's mother would have observed cryptically that Tansy was 'setting out her stall', in other words, putting her best foot forward to attract the male of the species.

'Will you be seeing him again, then,

this Emlyn Rees?' Once again Dinah kept her voice level and tried to sound casual.

'Oh, I doubt it. There's better fish in the sea. I prefer a man who knows how to treat a girl properly, not a clodhopper with mud on his boots.'

'I hope you find one around these parts, then.'

'Oh, I already have. When we were standing there arguing at the side of the road, who should come along on a racing bike but that Williams chap I've been fancying. He stopped when he saw us. 'Everything all right, Rees?' he says, and of course our Emlyn had to tip his cap to the gentry and say that it was. He stood there like a great lummox saying nothing until finally Philip — that's his name, Philip Williams — had to introduce himself. And you'll never guess what — I'm invited to a party at his house next Saturday.'

Poor Emlyn, Dinah mused, as they strolled in the direction of home. Of course he had to be circumspect, when this Philip was the son of his employer. He'd be afraid of losing his job if he spoke out of turn, and Tansy had probably embarrassed him with her flirting.

Feeling a warm glow inside her, Dinah finally admitted to herself that she fancied Emlyn Rees herself; had done so, in fact, since she first saw him striding across the field towards her. He'd obviously taken a shine to Tansy, but he must have seen through her by now. Did this mean that the way was now clear for Dinah? He obviously wasn't in a committed relationship with anyone, or he wouldn't have asked Tansy out . . .

So, what next? Dinah wouldn't dream of approaching him and asking him for a date, of course. All the women's magazines stressed that men preferred to take the lead in such matters. However, if they happened to meet, she could greet him politely, and perhaps make small talk. And she could spruce herself up a bit. Perhaps buy some material in a colour which would draw attention to her eyes, and make herself a new blouse.

The following morning, when the children were racing about outside at play time, Dora made an announcement.

'We've received an invitation, girls. I felt you'd want to take part, so I took the liberty of accepting on your behalf. Mrs Williams is giving a little soirée, as she put it, in honour of her sons, who will soon be leaving to join their regiments.'

'A farewell do?' Dinah asked.

'I suppose so, although Mrs Williams prefers to call it a leaving party.'

'Not much difference,' Tansy said, scowling.

'There is a great deal of difference, Miss Smith. As one with a husband in the Army, I can understand her feelings. The word 'farewell' has too much of a final ring to it — as if they won't be coming back.'

Tansy sniffed. Dinah realised that this

48

was probably the same function that Philip Williams had invited her to. Probably she'd been expecting a gathering of his friends, with dancing to the music of the gramophone.

Something exclusive, to which Dinah wasn't invited. Instead, they would all be standing around, drinking tea out of delicate china cups, exchanging meaningless words with the lady of the manor.

'It is kind of Mrs Williams,' Dora went on, 'to welcome us to Bryncollen in this way. She is also inviting the teachers from the local school, which will give us the chance to get to know them. Mr Evans has mentioned something about organising a few sports events for the children of both schools, to help our Soper Street lot fit in.'

'That's mighty big of him!' Tansy's tone was sour, and Dora glanced at her, puzzled.

'I don't think that's such a great idea,' Tansy grumbled. 'A sports day for Soper Street kids versus Bryncollen kids. It's just asking for trouble!'

'Why on earth?' Dora shook her head in disbelief. 'We've always taken part in inter-school sports. Surely you remember seeing the Challenge Cup in the assembly hall? The year we won that was one of our greatest triumphs as a school.'

'That was all very well, when we were up against other schools from Coventry. This is different. It's the Welsh against the English!'

'Oh, for goodness' sake! All that old enmity died down centuries ago. We're all part of Britain now, in case you haven't noticed. And the locals have done us proud, taking in so many evacuated children. Speaking for myself, I've been given a marvellous welcome by the Llewellyns. They couldn't be kinder if I was a cousin, or something.'

'Lucky for some,' Tansy muttered. Dinah smiled sympathetically. She had a pretty shrewd idea of the sort of welcome that Mari Matthews had dished out. At the same time, prickly

Tansy probably wasn't doing much to fit in there, either.

'In any case, it's all arranged,' Dora went on. 'There will be a football match, supervised by one of the Bryncollen teachers. If all goes well, it may be extended to form a league. A sports day was discussed, but Mr Evans feels that we should put that off for the moment, since the weather can be iffy at this time of year.'

'Nothing organised for the girls, then!' Tansy was determined to hang on to her grudge.

'Oh, yes. We'll have indoor games for all the children, with small prizes for the winner. I'm counting on you two to come up with some ideas. And Bryncollen has very active Cub and Brownie packs, and any of the older children who feel like joining will be encouraged to attend. In fact, I happen to know that some of our lot are already keen members at home. We might have to volunteer to help out, if the larger numbers prove too much for the present leaders to handle.'

'I was a Guide for a couple of years,' Dinah informed her.

'Good, then you already know the ropes. I'm sure that Brown Owl, or whatever they call her, will be at the Williams' party. You can have a chat about it then.'

Dinah was beginning to look forward to the party, although she'd suffered a disappointment in the matter of a new blouse. The one and only draper's shop could boast only a few small rolls of fabric, and nothing at all like the colourful cotton she had envisioned.

'We just can't get the things we'd like,' the owner had explained. 'Even when we do place an order we have to wait months before it comes in. Before the war we used to stock fabrics of all kinds, but now . . . '

'I see. I was hoping to have something new to wear when we go to a party this weekend, but that won't be possible now,' Dinah had said.

'Ah, Mrs Williams's tea party, I

suppose. I heard she was inviting the visiting school teachers. There's sad for her it is, sending her three boys off to the war.'

Dinah agreed that it was and the woman handed her a booklet.

'This may give you some ideas. It's all to do with Make Do and Mend, that slogan we're always hearing about.'

Dinah had thanked her and gone out, glancing down at the booklet as she went. She could see that if this beastly war went on for much longer, they would all end up looking very shabby indeed. Rationing seemed to be getting worse all the time, and even if one could get the coupons required, what was the use if the goods were simply not available?

One of the bright ideas described how to make a 'smart pullover'. You were supposed to cut up an old tweed skirt and turn the remnant into the lower half of a jersey. Then you used up oddments of wool to knit a 'gaily striped' top and sleeves, which had to be sewn onto the tweed.

'Good grief!' Dinah had said aloud, stuffing the paper into her jacket pocket. 'Dior would have a fit!'

However, help was at hand. A surprise was waiting for her when she returned home after school on Thursday.

'There's a parcel come for you, cariad,' Gwladys told her, beaming with joy to be the bearer of good news. 'Evans the post brought it just after you left this morning. Coventry, the postmark says.'

'It must be from Mum! I wasn't expecting anything.'

'There's lovely, cariad. Well, aren't you going to open it? I'm dying to see what's inside. Something soft, by the feel of it.'

Dinah struggled with the knots, not wanting to cut the string. Every self-respecting household kept a drawer filled with brown paper and string, to be used over and over again. At last the parcel was undone, revealing a royal blue blouse, which she held up against herself.

'There's lovely!' Gwladys said again. 'I wonder where she found that? Just look at those pearl buttons. Hard to find those are, nowadays.'

'I expect Mum made it for me herself, Mrs Richards. She's handy with her Singer sewing machine. And she has a big button box already.'

'She's thrifty, your Mam, then,' Gwladys said with obvious approval.

Dinah nodded, feeling a wave of nostalgia for Grandad's old cigar box, which had been the repository of Mum's button collection for years. Every time some garment was relegated to the rag bag the buttons were carefully cut off and kept for future use. Dinah and Joyce had spent many a happy hour playing with the contents on the rag rug in front of the fire.

She slipped up to her bedroom, eager to read the letter which had come with the blouse.

Would you believe I found this blouse on a stall in the market? Mum had written. *Never worn, by the look of it, but I'm not surprised because it was big enough to fit an elephant. Whoever owned it hadn't been able to pass it down to anyone else because of that. I snapped it up at once and cut it down for you. Joyce tried to get hold of it, of course, you know what she's like. Hands off, my girl, I said. This is for your sister. It's about time she had a turn.*

Tears came to Dinah's eyes as she read this. Good old Mum! Trust her to give someone else the benefit of her find, when she could have remade the blouse to fit herself. And of course it was one thing to make up a garment out of nice new fabric; quite another to have to unpick something and begin again.

The three teachers turned up at the Williams' home on Saturday, looking forward to the party. Dora was eager to see the inside of the house. Having come from a small terrace in Coventry she was curious to know how people coped with so much space.

Tansy was determined to enjoy herself to the full and as she confided to Dinah, if she didn't have a date with Philip Williams by the end of the evening, she'd eat her hat!

Dinah laughed, as she was meant to do, but she didn't reciprocate with comments about Emlyn Rees. The last thing she wanted was for the other girl to know about her feelings for the man. She wouldn't put it past Tansy to let something slip to Dora — or worse, to Emlyn himself.

Was she out of her mind? She had met the man once, and that encounter had been embarrassing, so why was she so keen to see him again? Bryncollen was a small place and she'd be certain to run into him again, especially since he was her landlady's nephew. What if he gave her the cold shoulder?

When the moment arrived, Dinah walked into the reception room with a dry mouth. A quick glance around showed her that Emlyn Rees hadn't arrived. Or perhaps he wasn't coming at all. Brian Williams probably didn't invite his employees to his social gatherings.

Disappointed, she murmured something to Sybil Williams, who was greeting each guest as they arrived. There was no sign of her husband but their three sons were lined up beside her, to be introduced in turn. Philip Williams barely glanced at Dinah, but his eyes brightened at the sight of Tansy. She was dressed conservatively with subdued make-up, but her hair was once again hanging loose, à la Veronica Lake. Before long he left the line and, ignoring his mother's compressed lips, he moved off with Tansy.

Dora was immediately swept away by two members of the Mothers' Union, which left Dinah standing alone. The local teachers hadn't turned up yet, so she had nobody to talk to. What was she supposed to do with her hands? Tea hadn't been served yet, so she didn't even have a cup and saucer to fiddle with. Why on earth had she come? But of course she knew the answer to that one. Mrs Williams had issued the royal command, and it would have been an insult to refuse.

'Hello — all alone, are you?' Paul, the eldest of the Williams' sons, had come up behind her, unnoticed.

'Um, yes,' she said, feeling foolish. Tansy would have countered with a bright remark, such as 'not now you're here', but Dinah didn't know how to flirt. Besides, he was simply doing his duty on seeing that a guest was floundering. Thankful though she was to be rescued, she soon tired of trying to look interested as he droned on about his recent walking holiday in Snowdonia. Not one question did he ask her about herself. Would this dreadful evening never end?

And then her heart gave an uncomfortable thump as Emlyn Rees appeared in the doorway.

'What do you think of Bryncollen?'

This was not the first time that Dora had been asked this question. What did they expect her to say in reply? She smiled at the stout matron who had been introduced to her as Edith Wilmott, president of the Mothers' Union. If she hated the place, good manners would hardly permit her to say so. 'Everyone has been most kind,' she said truthfully, 'and the scenery hereabouts is beautiful. I look forward to some pleasant walks, if the weather holds.'

'You should ask one of the Cubs to show you where to go. It will count as the daily good deed they're supposed to do. A stranger could easily become lost in the lanes, now that all the signposts have been removed,' Mrs Wilmott said gravely.

'And a real nuisance that is,' another woman remarked, 'but of course they had to do it in case spies manage to infiltrate the area. What's worse, though, is not having the gas lamps lit in the streets for fear the light attracts enemy bombers. I've taken to staying home rather than going out in the evenings, in case I come to grief.'

Dora frowned. 'But surely that isn't necessary here? I mean, that's why we've been evacuated to Bryncollen, so the children will be safe.'

'Ah!' Mrs Wilmott said. 'Who knows what that madman, Hitler, means to do next?' There was no reply to that of course and, having exhausted all conversation, Dora went to say goodbye to her hostess, and began the trek back to her lodgings.

Of course she missed Coventry. That was only to be expected. She loved the ancient city, with its historic buildings dating back to the Middle Ages. Unlike the other teachers, however, she wasn't leaving family members behind, for Jim was already away, serving in the Army. On the plus side she was able to continue with the job she loved, and she felt a sense of accomplishment at being still in the picture for her pupils.

Thinking of the thousands of children from Britain's cities who had gone among strangers, she felt as though her heart would break. She liked to believe that most of their host families would show kindness to the little ones in their care. Yet, human nature being what it is, there would surely be others who behaved differently towards the young cuckoos in their nests. Then, too, some of the older children might be difficult, particularly some who came from inner city areas, and then it would be the host families who suffered.

Thinking about it all she sighed. That Hitler had a lot to answer for!

Bryncollen, now; the people had welcomed the children with open arms. As far as she knew there had only been one problem, involving a set of twins, a boy and girl, five years old, who had been billeted in separate homes. Never having been separated in their lives, and used to sleeping together, they had wept inconsolably for days until Dora got together with the billeting officer and a household was found that could accommodate two youngsters.

She wished she could do something about Tansy Smith's landlady; a very difficult woman, by all accounts. She hesitated to intervene, for fear of making things worse. Still, Tansy was a grown woman, and not afraid of speaking her mind, so presumably she could look after herself.

Tansy Smith! Now that was rather odd. Where on earth had the girl disappeared to, and so soon after arriving at the Williams' gathering, too? She appeared to have been claimed by their youngest son — Philip, was it? — and hadn't been seen since.

And what about Dinah Blake? Another of the sons, a rather pompous individual, seemed to have taken it upon himself to chat to her. The girl was obviously doing her best to look interested, but by the look of things it was an uphill battle. Then the chap had been called away, and luckily one of the local teachers had claimed her after that. Even so, there was no sign of Dinah on the road ahead.

Mind your own business, Dora Ramsey she told herself. *They are two grown women, not your school children!*

★   ★   ★

Dinah, meanwhile, had suffered a disappointment. Emlyn Rees had barely noticed her when he strode in the reception room. He had apparently come to deliver a message to Paul Williams who, after a curt apology to Dinah, had left the house, with Emlyn in tow.

Even Mrs Williams barely acknowledged her stammered thanks when she left, but then the woman had a lot on her mind. Three sons would leave the family home this week, but how many would return?

When she reached the back door of her temporary home, she could hear voices inside; Gwladys must have company. Well, they could exchange greetings and then Dinah would go to her room and write a letter to her mum.

When she entered the kitchen, however, her heart skipped a beat at the sight of Emlyn Rees. He scrambled to his feet when she saw her.

'Ah, there you are, Miss Blake!' Gwladys said, smiling. 'This is our Emo, my sister's boy.'

'Actually we've met,' Emlyn said, holding out his hand. 'Sorry I couldn't stop to chat back there. There was a problem on the farm and Mr Paul was needed urgently, like.'

'I see.'

'Did you enjoy the evening? A bit stiff up there, aren't they?'

'Now, now, Emo. No need to be like that,' his aunt admonished.

'I was only wondering what Miss Blake thought of old Ma Williams, see, that's all,' he defended himself.

'She did seem a bit distracted, yes. And do call me Dinah.'

'Distracted is a good word for it,'

Emlyn said. 'Up to his old tricks again, is Master Philip.'

'What's he done this time?' Gwladys asked. 'Gambling, is it?'

'I wouldn't know about that, but it looks like he's getting involved with the English school teacher this time.'

'I thought you were walking out with her, boyo?' Gwladys asked.

'That's before I found out what she was like. A flighty piece, she was, not someone you could take home to Mam.'

'Sour grapes, is it? Threw you over for the son of the house, did she? Time you found yourself a nice girl, boyo . . . like Miss Blake here.'

Dinah blushed furiously. Studying his fingernails, Emlyn made no reply. At least he hadn't made a furious denial, which was something, she supposed. 'I have letters to write,' she said, standing up to leave.

'Oh, but stay and have a cup of tea, cariad,' Gwladys suggested, smiling. 'I was just about to make another pot.'

'No, thanks, Mrs Richards. I've already had two cups up at the house. I really must write and thank Mum for this blouse. I haven't had a minute until now.'

'Oh, yes, that lovely blouse. The colour really suits you, cariad. Don't you think so, Emo?'

Emlyn muttered something that might have been an agreement.

When Dinah had gone upstairs. Gwladys turned back to her nephew. 'Do you think she should be warned, boyo?'

'Who, Dinah Blake? What about?'

'Na, na. The other one. Pansy, or whatever her name is. You know what I'm talking about; that Philip Williams. There was that girl over Brynamman way. Got her into trouble, he did, and then refused to do right by her. He's no gentleman, that one.'

'Too much of a gentleman to wed a miner's daughter, by all accounts. Her father came to see old Williams and laid down the law, but that didn't get him anywhere. Threatened to have a word with the mine owner, did old Williams, and get the chap thrown out of work if he didn't go back to where he came from.'

'Never!'

'It's true enough. I had it from the cook up there, see. Bessie Probert, who was married to Da's cousin, Probert the shop, till he fell down the cellar steps and broke his neck.'

'Well, there's awful. Mind you, I still think that girl should be warned.'

'None of my business, auntie.'

When Emlyn had gone, Gwladys hauled herself to her feet and went upstairs. *More than one way to skin a cat*, she told herself, as she tapped on Dinah's door.

'There's something you should know,' she said, as she lowered herself into the sagging armchair beside the bed. 'It's your friend, Miss Smith, see? Well, she ought to be warned about that Williams chap before it's too late.'

'What do you mean?'

Gwladys launched into her story. Chewing on her thumbnail, Dinah listened. 'So it would be only Christian if you had a word with her, cariad.'

'Oh, I doubt she'd pay attention to me, Mrs Richards. Besides, she's got a good head on her shoulders. Anyway, he'll be leaving soon, and that will solve the problem, if indeed there is one.'

'All the more reason to speak up now, see? I know what it was like in the last war. Some young fellows would try to talk their sweethearts into going too far, saying they were going off to fight for king and country, and what if they got killed before they ever knew what it was like to be loved? Didn't they deserve a bit of comfort, like, they'd say. And then of course the poor girls found themselves left with a packet of trouble. Sometimes their chaps did get killed, see, and then the girls were left with fatherless babes to bring up. Is that what you want for your friend? You have a word with her, cariad.'

4

'Where did you get to after the party the other evening?' Dora asked, when she and Dinah were supervising the children's morning playtime. 'I didn't see you leave.'

'Oh, I wanted to get home early. I had letters to write.'

'I thought perhaps you and Miss Smith went off somewhere together.'

Dinah hesitated. 'I think she was with the youngest Williams brother.'

'Really? That was fast work.'

Dinah looked over her shoulder to make sure that Tansy wasn't nearby. Not that they could have been overheard if she had been. The children's shouts would have drowned out their words.

'Actually, Mrs Ramsey,' Dinah said anxiously. 'I'm in a bit of a dilemma. It's my landlady, you see.'

'She's not being unpleasant, I hope?'

'No, no. Nothing like that. Someone told her that Tansy was seeing that Mr Williams and, well, she thinks I should warn her off.'

'That's a bit odd, isn't it?'

'According to Mrs Richards, he's a bit of a womaniser. He's already got one girl into trouble, and his parents wouldn't let him take responsibility. The thing is, I really don't want to say anything to Tansy. It would make it sound as if I thought she's likely to fall into his arms.'

'I see what you mean. Well, if I know our Miss Smith, she won't do anything so silly. Apart from anything else, she has her career to think of. As for young Mr Williams, he'll be out of the picture soon enough. I don't think you should worry about this. I'm sure your landlady means well, but perhaps you shouldn't interfere in Miss Smith's business.'

'Thank you, Mrs Ramsey. I was afraid that Tansy would come down on

71

me like a ton of bricks if I spoke up.'
Dinah went off to ring the bell, to
summon the pupils back to class.

Dora sighed. Now the ball was in her
court. As the senior member of the trio
she felt responsible for the younger
teachers but, much like Dinah, she
hated to get involved. Perhaps she
should just keep a close eye on things
until the Williams boys went away. Of
course, they might agree to keep in
touch while he was gone.

It was just as well that Dinah had a
landlady who liked to gossip; perhaps
her own landlady, Sian Llewellyn,
would be a similar fount of information. If not, the president of the
Mothers' Union would have a vested
interest in the safety of the teachers.

★ ★ ★

Meanwhile, the subject of these specu-
lations had some interesting thoughts of
her own. Tansy Smith was the product
of a very ordinary home, the daughter

of decent, working-class parents. Sharing an overcrowded house with her parents, six brothers and sisters and an elderly grandmother, she had always felt destined for better things. The family home was less cramped now that four of her siblings had joined up, but even so, the prospect of being evacuated to Bryncollen had provided a welcome change.

True, lodging with Mari Matthews was a challenge, but Tansy meant to change that — just as soon as she could find someone else with an available room to rent.

Meanwhile, meeting the Williams brothers was a bonus. Philip was obviously very interested, and Peter, the quiet one, couldn't seem to keep his eyes off her. From what she had seen of the house and grounds, the family was very well-to-do, and she soon indulged in a fantasy of spending the rest of her days there.

How that should be accomplished she wasn't sure, but if she played her cards right there was no telling what might happen. Presumably the estate would be inherited in due course by Paul, the eldest brother, but surely the others would come in for something.

Tansy had learned very early in life that love and romance was not for her. The love that existed between parents and children, yes, she had been lucky there; poor though her parents were, they had done their best to bring up their children in a happy atmosphere.

The other kind, no. Time and again she had observed that romantic love didn't last. A girl got all starry-eyed over some man and married him. Within a year or so the babies had started to come, and then all the sweetheart stuff was lost beneath a welter of wet nappies, endless house-work and mounting bills.

When she thought of her poor mother, with her red, work-swollen hands, Tansy knew that she wanted something better for herself. She had said as much to her mother on one occasion.

'Well, you're a teacher, aren't you? That's a good job that could take you anywhere. You've had advantages I never had, my girl. It's up to you to make the most of them. Mind you, I don't like to think of you spending the rest of your days alone, and who's to look after you in your old age?'

'I'm not likely to end in the workhouse, Mum,' Tansy had assured her, but Nellie Smith had shaken her head.

'And what happens if you fall ill, or have an accident, say? How would you earn a crust then? My hope for you is that some decent chap will come along and sweep you off your feet some day.'

'As long as it's a decent chap with money behind him,' Tansy muttered, too quietly for Nellie to hear her. And if he turned out to be not so decent after all, money would smooth the path.

Tansy had been born plain Ann Smith, but she had begun calling herself Tansy when she first left home, as it sounded more exotic. Then she had learned how to make up her face, to make the most of her assets. She couldn't afford a huge wardrobe on her teaching salary, but she could dress with flair and be well groomed at all times.

She had borrowed a book on etiquette from the library and she knew which fork to use when faced with a meal of several courses. Not that there were many of those nowadays, of course — what with everything being rationed.

One sleepless night she thought about her future, and considered her options. She was sensible enough to realise that she had no hope of marrying into the aristocracy; she would never be a duchess. But she would opt for a man from the gentry or, failing that, someone whose family had made money somehow.

But the war had put a stop to her plans. All the men were either rushing to join the services, or were being called up. You might meet someone at a Red Cross dance or an officers' tea party but it was always a case of 'here today, gone tomorrow'. As far as Tansy was concerned, being shunted off to Wales was the last straw.

Then she had come across the Williams family, and everything changed. Three handsome men, and not one of them married! She had fancied the youngest one, Philip, but she'd soon seen through him. Only after one thing, and if the rumours were true, he wasn't slow to take advantage. There was no harm in stringing him along a bit, though.

'You will write to me, won't you, Tansy?' he'd pleaded. 'And what about a photo? I'll need one, just to show the other chaps I have a beautiful girl waiting for me back home.'

'I suppose I could write, if you promise to write back, but a photograph? I don't know about that,' she'd teased. 'How do I know you don't have a wallet full of snaps? I don't want to be just one in the crowd.'

'You're the only woman in my life, Tansy Smith. I swear it!'

She doubted that very much, but it was a start. She was pretty sure that Peter, the quiet one, would also like to correspond, but he was rather shy and might not like to ask. Would she be making herself cheap by making the offer? Then there was Paul, but she wasn't sure about him.

Her main stumbling block was Sybil Williams, who was likely to be the mother-in-law from hell. When they'd been introduced, the woman had looked Tansy up and down as if she was sizing her up as a future kitchen maid. Tansy had smiled sweetly, pretending not to notice, but inside she'd been seething. When Philip had dragged her off to the conservatory on the pretext of looking at a potted banana tree, his mother had seen what was going on.

'I don't think your mother is too pleased, Philip,' Tansy had murmured.

'Oh, you don't need to worry about her. She always looks like that. Grim is her middle name.'

'That's not a very nice thing to say

about your mother.'

'Mama and I understand each other.' He'd reached out and drawn her into his arms, but Tansy struggled free. 'Somebody might come.'

'Who cares?'

'I do, as it happens,' she'd said firmly. 'I have to be careful of my reputation. My job depends on it.'

'Pooh! A little school teacher,' he'd mocked. 'You don't want to do that all your life, do you?'

'Unlike you, I wasn't born with a silver spoon in my mouth.'

'You could join one of the women's services, you know.'

'That's a thought,' she said, as he took her into his arms again.

★ ★ ★

November came before they knew it, bringing with it cold mornings and endless days of relentless rain.

'Now I know why they call it Wet Wales,' Tansy grumbled, as she shook the drops off her umbrella. 'Look at me. I'm absolutely drenched. If I don't get pneumonia it will be a miracle!'

'And my shoes are letting in water,' Dinah mourned. 'I've tried making insoles out of cardboard, but it doesn't make a bit of difference.'

'Then we'll all have to be prepared, like the wise virgins in yesterday's Bible reading. Keep a spare pair of shoes here to change into when you arrive, and a towel as well, if you can find one. And while you're at it, see if you can round up some books or old magazines for the children to look at. They can't go out to play in weather like this.'

Dinah groaned. The morning and lunch time breaks had been designed for a purpose. Unless the youngsters could let off steam in the the middle of the day they were impossible to teach in the afternoon. She might as well let the little ones put their heads down on their desks and go to sleep.

A letter from her mum cheered her up.

Don't worry if you don't hear from me for a while, Alice Blake wrote. *Your Gran hasn't been very well, so I'm off to Leamington to give her a hand. It's nothing to worry about, just a cold on the chest, but at her age we can't be too careful. I have a few days coming to me from work, so I may as well use them for this.*

On the way home from school Dinah popped into the newsagent's to find a greetings card to send to the old lady, but there was nothing.

'They're just not making things like that nowadays,' she was informed by the plump woman who kept the shop. 'Luxuries, see. Look, even the magazines have shrunk in size. There's a shortage of paper, see. What I do have is a nice diary, the sort with just the month and the date, no days of the week. Pre-war stock, that is. Why don't you take one for yourself? Or keep it by you, to give to somebody for Christmas.'

Dinah shook her head. 'I'm a bit short of cash at the moment. All I wanted was a nice card to cheer my Nan up while she's in bed.'

'What about a nice picture postcard? Lovely views of Bryncollen, see! What about this one, with the sheep? Show your mam that Wales isn't all coal mines, see.'

Having accepted her cards without a bag to put them in, Dinah put them away inside her book bag. Scurrying along with her head down against the driving rain, she felt a cloud of gloom descending on her. Life was bland, boring and predictable.

But all that changed in the middle of the month.

★ ★ ★

'I see Coventry's got it,' Evans the Post shouted from over the street.

'Got what?' Dora asked.

'Coventry. There's been a big air raid,' he explained. 'The news is all over the papers, see.'

Dora felt sick. She'd always known it was only a matter of time before Coventry was hit; any city within range of the Luftwaffe's bombers was in danger, not just poor London. But it was one thing to hear about damage in other places, quite another to see one's home town in jeopardy. Coventry was an ancient city, with many beautiful buildings, some dating from the Middle Ages. She hoped that the damage wasn't too bad.

The news had also reached Tansy and Dinah. 'We've got to find out how bad it is!' Tansy cried, when the three teachers met on their way into the school. 'My whole family is there, not to mention the children's parents. I'm going to Coventry on the next train.'

'You'll do no such thing!' Dora told her. 'In the first place, our duty is to the children here. We must carry on as usual — and please, don't breathe a word of this to any of them. There is absolutely no point in allowing them to worry — or at least, not until we know more.'

'But what are we going to do?'

'We'll carry on as usual, Miss Smith. There will probably be something about it on the wireless this evening. Then we can ring up to see what else we can find out.'

'But my landlady isn't on the phone!' Tansy wailed.

'But Mr Pepper is. I shall telephone him this evening. Being in the Home Guard, he's bound to have the latest news.'

'Then go and ring him now,' Tansy pleaded, but Dora shook her head.

'No, I shan't do that. I'm sure he's out and about, um, doing what he can.' She had almost said 'picking up the pieces' but where bombing was involved that expression had unpleasant connotations. Instead, she pointed out that the children were beginning to straggle in, and the school day was about to start.

But when the women tried to contact

Coventry that evening, using the phone booth at the end of Chapel Row, they were unable to get through. Time and again they heard the busy signal, and had to press button B to get their coppers returned.

'It's this beastly phone!' Tansy groaned. 'There must be something wrong with it. You'd better get on to Faults, Mrs Ramsey.'

'I'm afraid the trouble must be at the other end,' Dora explained patiently. 'I expect the lines are down, or something. I'm going home for my tea. I'll try again in the morning.'

'How can you even think of eating at a time like this? I'm staying right here until I get through!'

'I think we'd all do better to sit by the wireless, Miss Smith, rather than hanging about here in the cold. The BBC will give us the full story as soon as they can. Come along now, girls, chin up!'

Reluctantly, Tansy and Dinah trailed off towards their billets, Dinah to

Gwladys Richards' sympathy and her colleague to endure the gloomy remarks of Mari Matthews. There was nothing they could do but wait.

★　★　★

The news, when it did come, was bad. Coventry's city centre was devastated. Thousands of houses were damaged or destroyed, and factories were razed. Reports of casualties changed from hour to hour, as the death toll mounted and the hospitals overflowed with the injured.

There were reports of people from many miles away having seen the night sky lit up a fearful red as Coventry reeled beneath the firestorm.

The three teachers met for a council of war. 'I have discussed this with Mr Evans,' Dora said, 'and we think it best if I go to Coventry to assess the situation. By now the children have heard about the tragedy and every one of them is anxious to know if their parents are all right.'

'We must all go, of course!' Tansy pushed.

'No, Miss Smith. You're needed here. You and Miss Blake will have to divide up my class between you, and manage until I return.'

'It's not fair! Why should you be the one to go?' Tansy cried. 'You don't even have anyone there, like we do.'

'I'll ignore that remark,' Dora retorted stiffly. 'Mr Evans believes that I should go because I'm Acting Head. Coventry is in turmoil, and the powers-that-be must be overwhelmed with enquiries. They are more likely to respond to someone in authority, who has a more pressing need for information. I shall explain that we want news of the children's parents, so we can set their minds at ease.'

'If things are that bad, what makes you think they'll tell you anything? You're going on a wild goose chase, Mrs Ramsey. At least if I went — and Dinah, too, of course — we could go to our homes and see for ourselves if our mums are all right.'

'And that is what I intend to do on your behalf. In fact, I have the register with the children's addresses in it, and I shall visit each home in turn. I know that the mothers will be delighted to have news of their little ones. It's all settled. I'm off first thing in the morning, so if you have anything you'd like me to deliver for you, make sure I get it in time.'

Dora went back to her lodgings with a heavy heart. She wasn't looking forward to seeing the devastation that the enemy forces had wrought on her beloved city. And who was to say that the Luftwaffe wouldn't return to have another go? She almost wished she had given in to Tansy to take her place, but her duty was clear. If any of her pupils were now orphans, attempts would have to be made to contact any surviving relatives.

Her imagination ran riot. Visions ran through her fevered mind of mothers dying in hospital, begging for their children to be brought to the bedside for a last farewell. In such a case, would it be best for the child to return to Coventry, or to remain in safety in Wales? Would she be haunted by her decision in later years?

'Oh, do pull yourself together, Dora Ramsey!' she snapped, alarming a passing dog who thought her loud tone was directed at him. 'I'm going batty!' she chided herself silently, but deep down, she wondered how anyone could manage to stay sane among all this madness.

★　★　★

Dora was sitting in the home of Mr Pepper's niece, where the former headmaster was staying for the duration. Polly Steele had pressed a steaming cup of tea into the teacher's shaking hand and now Dora was trying to absorb everything she had seen and heard.

'Soper Street is gone,' Mr Pepper began. 'At least the school was empty at the time; we can be grateful for that. After you left it was taken over for a first aid post, but there was nobody on duty there that night. All hands were occupied, trying to put out the fires and digging people out.' His voice faltered. 'You remember Mattie, who cleaned the school? Well, she's gone, poor soul. I saw her myself, lying in the street. At least I was able to say a prayer over her and put down her skirts so she was decent.'

Shaken, Dora gazed into the fire, trying to collect her thoughts. Her own home was gone; the house where she had spent all of her married life was now a pile of bricks and shattered rafters. Rented, of course; at least they hadn't suffered the loss of something they owned. They'd given up the house when she went to Wales, and the furniture had been dispersed among friends and neighbours, on loan. What had become of it now? She would not waste this visit on going to find out. Her few valuables

— important documents, her late mother's cameo brooch and her father's medals from the Great War — were safely down in Wales. At least she had that consolation.

'You can stay here tonight, Mrs Ramsey,' Polly said.

'That's very kind, but I don't want to put you out.'

'It's no trouble. It'll only be a camp bed in the front room, mind, but you'll not find anywhere else. People are dossing down in school halls and churches. Anywhere to be in out of the cold.'

'Polly's already putting up some of the fire brigade,' Mr Pepper explained. They're on duty all night, but they have to find somewhere to sleep by day. A lot of them have been bombed out of their own homes.'

'I'll be grateful for anything. I shan't stay longer than I have to. I've promised Miss Smith and Miss Blake that I'll check on their people, and I mean to visit every one of our pupils' parents.

The children were told I was coming and most of them have sent drawings and little notes for them. One little boy even wanted me to bring his breakfast egg. 'She loves a fresh-boiled egg, does my mum, and I want her to have this one, from a Welsh chicken.' That's what he said. Wasn't that sweet?'

'I'm afraid it will take more than a boiled egg to comfort some of these parents,' Mr Pepper remarked. 'Homes and livelihoods gone for a lot of them. Whole streets wiped out, factories smashed, shops gone. I don't know where they're going to put everybody, I really don't.'

'At least they know their kiddies are safe in Wales,' Polly told him sadly. 'I know I would be. When you think about the fuss some of them made when this evacuation talk started, they'll be jolly glad you talked them into changing their minds, Uncle Bob.'

'Do you remember Mark and Bridie Samson, Mrs Ramsey?'

'Of course. They were both in my

class at one time.'

'Both gone. Their house took a direct hit. Their mother had put them under the kitchen table during the raid, but it didn't help, poor little souls.'

'I can't bear it!' Polly cried. 'That wicked, evil Hitler! Making war on innocent little children. Why does he do it? Is he out of his mind?'

'He's very much in it, as far as I can see, my girl. This is all part of his plan to subdue us. He's trying to destroy our morale, that's what, but if he thinks he can wear us down, he's very much mistaken. He's taken on the British now, and we'll never surrender!'

'And people like my Henry are going to give him as good as he gets!'

'Henry is your husband?' Dora queried.

'Yes, he's in the Royal Air Force, and I'm that proud of him!'

'I'm sure you are, dear. My husband is in the Army, even though he didn't need to go, because of his age. And Mr Pepper here is in the Home Guard, so that Hitler can jolly well mind his P's and Q's!'

★ ★ ★

Even fired up with patriotism from the evening before, the euphoria didn't last. The next morning, when she was walking through the streets with the acrid smell of soot and ash in her nostrils, Dora was filled with sadness as she thought of the suffering of the people of Coventry.

'Do you know where I can find the Smiths?' she asked a passing WVS worker, having gone to Tansy's street first. 'I'm a colleague of their daughter, and I promised her I'd see how they were faring.'

The woman consulted her clipboard. 'I believe they lived at number five. There's not much of it left now, I'm afraid.'

'But the people? I understand they're quite a big family.'

'Fortunately nobody was at home

when the raid began, with the exception of the grandmother. The others were scattered here and there, and I suppose they took shelter where they could. I've spoken to Mrs Smith, so I know this for a fact. She's gone to work as usual this morning; that's if there's any work left to go to.'

'And the old lady?' Dora asked in trepidation.

'She was alive when they pulled her out of the rubble but I can't tell you how she's faring now. You'll have to enquire at the hospitals.'

Dora's next stop was at Dinah's home. The house was still intact but there was no answer when she rapped at the door. A harrassed neighbour wanted to help, but had no useful information to share.

'All I know is Mrs Blake went to see her mother, who's poorly. I don't think she's back yet. As for that girl, Joyce, she works shifts on the buses, and I've no idea what time she'll be home.'

Dora thanked the woman and started

on her rounds to speak to the pupils' parents. She soon found that this was something of a lost cause because so many of the women worked outside the home. In cases where the houses had survived, she just had to surmise that the occupants had also come through unscathed.

When she did find anyone at home, she was welcomed with open arms. Little Billy Armstrong's mother listened to Dora's account of her son's progress with tears in her eyes.

'To think he wanted me to have his egg,' she sobbed. 'Now isn't that just like the child? Always thinking of other people before himself.'

'It's a tribute to the way you've brought him up, Mrs Armstrong.'

'It's kind of you to say so, Mrs Ramsey. Oh, I miss the little chap, I do really. For two pins I'd have fetched him back long before now, but after all we've just been through, I'm that glad I didn't.'

'Other mums will be feeling the same

way, I expect,' Dora comforted.

'I don't know if you heard, Mrs Ramsey, but the Samsons bought it. When I think of how Susan made a fuss about keeping her kiddies here in Coventry it just makes me want to weep. 'If the worst happens we'll all go together', that's what she told me, Mrs Ramsey. And she got her wish!' Mrs Armstrong began to sob.

Dora put her arm round the other woman's shaking shoulders. 'Can I make you a cup of tea before I go? You've had a nasty shock.'

'You'll have to make it with cold water, then, I'm afraid. There's no gas to heat it with.' Mrs Armstrong broke into a fresh round of sobs.

'Then if there's nothing more I can do, I'll be on my way. I'm afraid I have a long list of people to see before I go back to Wales.'

'You give my love to my boy then, Mrs Ramsey. Tell him his mum is well, and thinking of him all the time.'

'I'll do that, dear, certainly. Do try to

write to him if you can spare the time. The children love to get letters from home and one of us will be glad to read it to him, if he can't manage all the big words by himself.'

Her work done, Dora found that she had some hours before her train went, so she went to have a look at the cathedral. Dedicated to the archangel Michael, the beautiful structure had stood there since the fourteenth century, an inspiration to all who visited it.

The tears ran down her cheeks unchecked as she surveyed the ruin in front of her. St Michael's had survived the Civil War, when Cromwell's Army had wrought havoc on so many of England's old churches, but now the Luftwaffe had brought it down in one night. Only the outer walls and the spire remained now.

As Dora knew, there was a legend surrounding St Michael, who had slain a dragon. Or did that mean that he had vanquished the Devil? She wasn't sure. Whatever it was, England needed his help now. The words of an old prayer came into her mind, and she mouthed the words as she turned away. 'Holy Michael, Archangel, defend us in the day of battle. Be thou our safeguard against the wickedness and snares of the devil . . . '

* * *

Dora had the unhappy task of telling her colleagues what she had learned as soon as she returned to Wales. 'As far as I could tell, Miss Smith, your family are well, except your grandmother, who is in hospital.'

'But she's going to be all right, isn't she?' Tansy fretted.

'I'm afraid I was wasn't able to find out. The hospitals are in a terrible state, as you might imagine. Patients lying on cots and mattresses in the corridors and everything in a turmoil. Mr Pepper has promised to check with the Red Cross and the WVS and any other relief organisation he can think of, and he'll let you know.' Dora tried to soothe her. 'Of course, I daresay you'll hear from your mother before that happens. She's bound to realise how worried you must be.'

'And what about my sister?' Dinah asked. 'I know that Mum was safe in Leamington when the raids came, but Joyce couldn't go with her because she had to work.'

'Well, your house is still standing and your neighbour seemed to think that Joyce was safe, and that's all I know at the moment.'

'What about the children?' Tansy wondered. 'Are you going to make an announcement at Assembly?'

'I'm going to chat to each one separately,' Dora told them. 'Fortunately their mothers seem to have come through safely, except for a few who have had to go to hospital with injuries which are not life-threatening. Most of their fathers weren't even in Coventry at the time, of course, because they're away in the forces. I do have a bit of news they'll want to hear, though . . . the old school is gone, smashed to smithereens.'

Tansy managed a smile. 'They'll love to hear that! Are we going to tell them about the poor kiddies who died in the air raid?'

'I don't think so, do you? If they ask specifically, of course, we can't lie to them. We'll just hope that it doesn't occur to them.'

'And if they ask about their homes? What will we tell them?'

'We shall change the subject,' Dora said firmly. 'I don't want to give them nightmares. We are fairly safe here and I want to keep that illusion.'

'Illusion?' Dinah faltered. 'Do you think there might be bombs here after all, Mrs Ramsey?'

'It's doubtful, Miss Blake. I expect that Hitler is directing his Luftwaffe to places where there is a greater concentration of people and buildings, as well as docks, airfields and factories. He'll want to do as much damage as possible to important facilities, at the same time trying to bring down morale. What is there to target at Bryncollen?'

★ ★ ★

After school, Dinah returned to the house, carrying a pile of exercise books. Never before had she felt less like marking compositions. She had supervised some of the older children while Dora was away, and she had given them these essays to write. Coming up with a suitable topic hadn't been easy; all the old chestnuts seemed inappropriate now.

What I did in my holidays. Who could go on holiday in wartime? *What I want to be when I grow up.* Would these children survive to reach adulthood? *My family.* Would families ever be the same again, with fathers going off to war, and mothers being bombed out of their homes?

Telling herself not to be so defeatist, she had finally settled on *Why we shall win the war* and the children had set to with alacrity, especially the boys. She had a shrewd idea that they'd written reams about bombs, guns, and other weapons of war.

When she reached the house, there was nobody at home. She put the kettle on, intending to make herself a cup of tea; Mrs Richards had assured her that it was all right for her to do so, as long as she didn't go mad with the sugar ration. Not that Dinah needed telling. Everyone knew that if you went out to tea, or even just dropped in to see a friend, you took a pinch of sugar with you in a twist of paper.

She was just heating the pot when she heard the back door open and a voice call out, 'Anyone home?'

Emlyn Rees! She patted her hair down, wishing she had thought to put on lipstick when she'd left school.

'Oh, prynhawn da! Miss Blake, isn't it?'

'Good afternoon, Mr Rees,' she said politely.

'Auntie not at home?'

'No, I'm afraid not.'

'Oh, well, it was nothing important. Just passing by, I was, and thought I'd say hello, see.'

As he turned to leave, Dinah amazed herself by suggesting that he stay for a cup of tea. 'It'll be ready in two shakes.'

'Diolch yn fawr! Just a little milk, please, and no sugar,' he said.

'Given it up for the war effort?' Dinah said, smiling. 'Sugar, I mean.'

'Na, na, I never took it. I give my ration to our mam, see. She uses it to make cakes. I like a nice bit of cake, I do.'

'I'm afraid I can't offer you any to go with your tea. I don't like to help myself when Mrs Richards isn't in.'

'There might be a biscuit in that tin up on the shelf. You can tell Auntie Gwlad that I was the thief, see, and she won't give you a row.'

For a moment they sipped their tea in companionable silence, and then he said abruptly, 'Everything all right with your family back in Coventry, is it? I was at the pictures and I saw the damage on the newsreel, see. There's terrible it is, all those people dead, and half the town down in rubble.'

'I think so. Apparently our house is still in one piece, and I know Mum is all right. She's still in Leamington with my nan. I'm a bit worried about Joyce, though. That's my sister. According to Mrs Ramsey, our neighbours don't know where she is, either.'

'What does she do for a living?'

'The last I heard, she was a conductress on the buses, but knowing our Joyce, she could have thrown that up and started something else.'

'Perhaps she had call-up papers and went to join up.'

'Not without telling Mum,' Dinah replied.

'Never you mind. She's probably turned up by now, see. When your mam gets back to Coventry she'll write and give you all the news.' He suddenly looked awkward and added, 'I don't suppose you'd care to — '

He was interrupted by the arrival of his aunt, who greeted him with delight and their conversation lapsed into Welsh, which Dinah couldn't follow, so she left them to it and went upstairs. She could cheerfully have thumped Mrs Richards, fond though she'd become of the woman. What a moment to arrive! Surely Emlyn had been about to ask her out, but there was nothing she could do about it now.

Tansy, now, was made of sterner stuff. She would probably have watched for Emlyn to leave, followed him out, and reminded him he wanted to ask her something! Sadly, Dinah could not do the same. Her mother had always stressed that men did not like girls who ran after them — literally or otherwise.

She opened the first exercise book. *We are going to win the war because Mister Church Hill says so. We are going to make a lot of big bombs and drop them on that man Ittaler.*

She grinned, 'That's the spirit, Ronnie Tatler!'

* * *

Meanwhile, life carried on much as it usually did in Bryncollen. Dinah did her best to simply get on with things, busying herself with day-to-day matters, and eventually the long-awaited letter from her mother arrived.

I am very worried about your sister, her mum wrote. *She hasn't come home, and nobody seems to know where she is. I went to the bus depot and spoke to the manager and he told me that she didn't report for work on the morning before the raid. Quite cross about it he was, too, saying it upset his schedule and he had to bring someone back from their day off. He said unless she reported back to work toot sweet (I don't think I've spelled that right!) then she can forget about the job.*

Doesn't she know there's a war on?

Of course, what was I meant to think after that? I went round to see Pam Willis, that friend she used to go to the hops with, but Pam doesn't know anything either. Then I tried the hospitals, but no help there. They have people there who are still unconsious. or too shocked to say anything and nobody knows who they are. What about their identity cards, then, I said, but that was silly, of course. Women lost their hand-bags in the bombing, and some poor souls were already in bed when their homes collapsed under them.

So there we are. No Joyce. I'm sorry to burden you with this, love, but I'm that worried. If you hear anything you will let me know, won't you? I keep hoping that somehow she's gone down there to stay with you, but I suppose that's not possible.

5

Tansy marched up to the Williams' house, not caring that the rain was coming down in sheets. Her shoes were leaking, but she scorned the homespun remedy that she had known from childhood; making an insole out of cardboard. These needed to go to the cobbler, but what was she supposed to wear in the meantime? She needed new shoes, but finding something suitable in the shops when there was a war on was like searching for gold in a bale of straw. The last time she had gone looking the assistant had offered her a pair of plimsolls, for goodness' sake, which was all they had in her size!

Tansy was vain about her shoes. That came from having to wear other people's cast-offs when she was young. Other children might come to school on the first day of the autumn term wearing shiny new footwear, but not Tansy Smith — or Ann, as she was known back then. Her worst year was when she'd inherited her brother Michael's shoes, all trodden down at the back because he was too lazy to undo the laces before shoving his feet into them. Needless to say other, luckier, children mocked her for this, calling her gypsy, tinker, and worse names than that.

Looking up at the house in the distance, Tansy knew that this was the sort of environment she wanted for herself. She wanted a home and a family, and she was determined not to settle for a hand-to-mouth existence in the backstreets of Coventry. If there were any backstreets still standing! She had seen her mother ground down by overwork and poverty, and she wanted a better life for herself. For the moment she had a good job and a reasonable salary as a teacher, but under normal circumstances married women weren't allowed to teach, and she was determined not to slide back into obscurity.

Marriage to one of the Williams sons would save her from that, and she would never have another opportunity as good as this. Their mother would be a stumbling block, of course — but she wouldn't last forever. And now that Philip was her regular escort, Tansy had a foot in the door.

The maid answered the door, looked down her nose at Tansy. 'Yes?'

'I've come to see Mister Philip.'

'Well, he isn't here,' the woman replied snootily.

'Do you know when he'll be back?' Tansy asked, trying to be polite.

The girl shrugged. 'Gone off to join his regiment, or whatever it is.'

'Then I'll speak to one of his brothers.'

'Mister Paul ain't here, neither.'

'Presumably Mister Peter is? Kindly let him know I'd like to see him.'

'Wait here.'

Left fuming on the doorstep, Tansy

wondered if she'd made a mistake in coming. What if the insolent little maid fetched Mrs Williams to the door, and the old girl asked Tansy to state her business? She heard footsteps approaching, and braced herself.

'Miss Smith! What on earth are you doing, standing out here in the rain? I swear I'd give that idiot girl her marching orders if it wasn't so hard to find decent servants nowadays. All the girls are going into factories, or joining up. Well, come in, come in!'

Peter Williams wasn't as tall as his brothers, and his hairline was receding. Still, he had kind brown eyes and a pleasant expression.

'Actually it was Philip I came to see,' Tansy told him. 'But the maid tells me he's not here.'

'No, indeed. Didn't she tell you? He received his orders and he's already gone. Paul, too. Here, let me have that wet mac and you can come and sit by the fire.'

'Mrs Williams . . . '

'Oh, Mother's not here. She's out on Women's Institute business or something. Would you like a cup of coffee?'

'Yes, please.'

'Hang on a mo, then. I'll go and rustle some up.'

While he was gone, Tansy stared around her. There were some very nice paintings on the wall. 'I bet those didn't come from Woolworth's,' she told the dog, who stood up and sniffed her hand. She wasn't used to dogs and flinched slightly.

'Lie down, Ben!' Peter told the animal, who gave a heavy sigh and returned to the fireside. 'Don't worry about old Ben,' he said. 'He's a gentle soul. Thirteen now, and I've had him since he was a pup. Are you getting warmed up now? The coffee will be here in a minute and that'll soon put you right.'

'I would have thought that Philip would let me know he was off to the Army before he left,' Tansy complained.

'Oh, that's Philip for you. He never

was any good at farewells.'

'He promised to write to me, though.'

'Did he?' Peter looked rather doubtful. 'I shouldn't put too much faith in that, if I were you. I mean, he'll be pretty busy when he gets there, drilling and all that.'

It was an awkward moment, and Tansy was glad of the interruption when the maid came in, carrying a tray with a silver coffee pot and two cups and saucers.

'I'd better be on my way,' Tansy said regretfully, once she had swallowed the last delicious drop.

'I'll walk down with you,' Peter said. 'Ben hasn't had a walk yet today. You don't mind, do you?'

'No, I'll be glad of the company.'

Strolling down the drive, Tansy indulged in a fantasy about life in the future. She was out walking with her husband and his dog. The war was over, and they were all about to live happily ever after.

What about Peter Williams? He didn't have the sophistication of his elder brother, or the smouldering charm of Philip, but he was a very eligible man in his own right.

'I expect to be leaving soon, myself,' Peter said.

'Oh? How is it that you didn't leave when your brothers went?'

'Because I'm joining the RAF. I want to be a pilot.'

'Really! Have you ever flown before?'

'Oh, yes. When I was up at Oxford I belonged to a flying club and I managed to get my licence. I've been keeping an eye on the political situation, you see, and I was pretty sure that war was coming. I wanted to prepare myself.'

'But won't that be dangerous?' Tansy asked anxiously.

Peter smiled at her. 'Tell me what isn't dangerous in these times! Why, even civilians are being drawn into this wretched war. You of all people should know that, coming from Coventry.'

'That's true.'

'Is your family still there? Are they all right?' Peter looked concerned.

'That's a matter of opinion. Our house is gone, and my grandmother is in hospital, and goodness only knows where the others are living.'

'I'm so sorry to hear that.'

His voice sounded quite genuine and Tansy nodded her thanks. 'Still, we're no worse off than many other families, I suppose,' she said sadly.

They had arrived at the Matthews house, and stood chatting for a moment before Peter said goodbye and strode off, with Ben at his heels.

A movement of the lace curtains at the front window told Tansy that she was being watched. Sure enough she was accosted by Mrs Matthews as soon as she came through the door. The woman was enveloped in her usual flowered overall, and curlers peeped from beneath the duster that served as a turban.

'Getting your hooks into that Peter

Williams now, I see,' she snapped.

'I beg your pardon?'

'You heard what I said. I saw you, loitering out there with him. As if it's not bad enough you've been traipsing all over Bryncollen with that Philip Williams, and he's no better than he should be, never mind courting the brother as well.'

'I'm not courting anyone, Mrs Matthews. Philip is a friend, that's all.'

'I know different. First you went out with poor Emlyn Rees and you threw him over. Then it was that Philip, now it's the brother. This is a respectable house, Miss Smith, and I've got the chapel to think of. I'll have no hussy living under my roof. Unless you mend your ways I'll have to ask you to leave.'

'I am not a hussy!' Tansy bawled. 'This is ridiculous! Peter was simply seeing me home.'

'So you say. Well, I'll tell you what I think, shall I, Miss Smith? It's my belief you fancy yourself as mistress of that grand house. Perhaps you can worm your way in there, you with your fancy city ways and the way you paint your face to ensnare honest men. A marriage of convenience, isn't that what they call it? But it will do you no good in the end.'

'I don't know what you're talking about.'

'It's in the Bible, see? Better is a dinner of herbs where love is, than a fatted ox and hatred with it. Proverbs chapter fifteen, verse seventeen.'

Tansy stalked out of the room, slamming the door behind her.

6

Christmas was fast approaching. 'We must make sure it's a special time for the children,' Dora said. 'After all, it's their first Christmas away from home, and they're bound to be missing their parents and all the usual traditions in their homes, whatever those may be.'

Dinah looked a little blank. 'I somehow thought we'd all be going home for the holidays.'

'Really, Miss Blake! How did you suppose we were going to manage that? This isn't a boarding school, you know. And even if we could, what do some of them have to go back to, with so many houses bombed out? Apart from that, what was the point of evacuating the school if we took them back into danger now?'

'I wouldn't put it past that Hitler to make a special effort over Christmas,'

119

Tansy said. 'Although I don't know what the point would be in the Luftwaffe returning to Coventry, if things are as bad as you say.'

'Ladies, please! The point is, we're here now, and we have to celebrate the season as best we can, for the children's sake, if not our own. Now, I thought a carol service in the church, and on the last day of term, a party at school.'

'That'll be a madhouse, with everyone milling about in the parish hall,' Tansy pointed out. 'Why not have individual parties in the classrooms, with games and eats?'

'That sounds like a good idea, I'll see if the Women's Institute can provide the food, even if it is only Spam sandwiches.'

Dinah had been thinking. 'I know that some of the little ones are worried, in case Father Christmas won't be able to find them here. They've been asking me if he knows they've left Coventry. Of course I told them that he knows what he's doing, but what if he doesn't?

We can't let that happen to them.'

'Don't tell me you still believe in Father Christmas,' Tansy mocked.

'You know what I mean! What if some of the parents aren't able to send presents, or they get lost in the post? You know it's not reliable at the moment. I couldn't bear it if any of my little ones woke up on Christmas morning with nothing in their stockings.'

'We'll have to monitor the arrival of parcels coming in the post,' Dora decided. 'Then if it looks as if some poor child is going to be left out, we can step into the breach. I don't know how we'll manage that, but there's no point in worrying until we know more.'

Dora called at the post office, asking to see the postmaster. He was an elderly man, resentful at having been brought out of retirement. He greeted her sourly, scratching his balding head while she explained her mission. 'I don't know what you think I can do, Missus.'

'Well, I thought that you could hold

back any parcels addressed to the evacuees, and I — or one of the other teachers — will collect them until we see if any child has been left out.'

'Na, na, Missus! That won't do at all. Tampering with the Royal Mail, that would be, see and punishable with a fine, that is.'

'But surely in this case . . . ?'

'Na, na. Evans the Post will deliver parcels all round the houses as usual, and that's my last word on it, see.'

'But some of the kiddies still believe in Father Christmas. That will all be spoiled if they see brown paper parcels coming from Coventry.'

'Then more fool you for encouraging them in pagan superstitions,' said the stalwart of the Bethesda chapel.

Dora tried again. 'All right, then. I'm asking you to hold the parcels back, just for a few hours. One of us will come and look at the parcels, just to see who they're addressed to.'

'Against Post Office regulations, Missus.'

'Oh, have it your own way, you heartless little man!' Dora rushed out of the post office, biting back a few choice words which definitely would not go down well with the chapel-goers.

'This is such a nuisance,' she said, when she returned to her colleagues, having to confess to defeat. 'We'll just have to ask the hostesses to let us know if and when parcels arrive.'

'And how do you propose to contact them about this?' Tansy demanded. 'Make an announcement in the church and the chapels? That will let the cat out of the bag, good and proper!'

'You're right, of course, Miss Smith. Well then, one of us will have to go from door to door and speak to each one personally.'

'You can count me out. I've promised the vicar I'll go out looking for holly and ivy to decorate the church.'

'How on earth will you manage that? You don't know the district very well, and you don't want to be accused of trespassing.'

'Peter Williams has promised to take me. We're going out this Saturday, just to see where the best bits are, then if he gets called up before Christmas I'll know where to go.'

'I hope you wear wellies this time, then,' Dinah said mildly. 'As I recall, you missed a nice country walk before when you were tottering around on your high heels.'

'Just for that remark you can go rapping on doors, Miss Nosy!'

'I'll be glad to,' Dinah told her, but when she'd had time to think, she realised that she didn't relish the prospect at all.

'I don't know most of those people,' she told her landlady. 'When they see me coming they'll think I'm selling something, and won't open the door. And what if they speak Welsh to me? I shan't know what to do.'

Gwladys Richards laughed. 'Then ask our Emo to go with you, cariad. Everyone knows him.'

'Oh, I couldn't!'

'But I can! Look, I'm going over to have tea with our Bron tomorrow. I'll leave a message with her.'

Thrilled, Dinah went upstairs to look over her meagre wardrobe. Should she try to dress up a bit, in the hope of making herself more attractive to him, or would that be too obvious? Her mother's words came back to her, as if she were in the room with her. *Just be yourself.*

That was it, then. Plain Dinah Blake she would be.

* * *

When she heard about this expedition, Dora was pleased. The young teacher was too quiet for her own good. Getting out in public with a personable young man was just what she needed. Tansy Smith, on the other hand, seemed to be actively pursuing the Williams brothers; first Philip, and now Peter. It was to be hoped that it wouldn't end in tears.

Her colleagues seemed so young to

Dora, who was fast approaching forty. How long ago it seemed since she had first set eyes on Jim Ramsey, a good-looking, dark-haired, lanky sort of boy. It was unbelievable to think that they'd been married for sixteen years. There hadn't been any grand passion and her failure to conceive children had been a sorrow to them both, but it had been a good enough marriage in its way, nevertheless.

Poor Jim — where was he now? Dora had written faithfully every Sunday but there had never been any word from him. She hoped that he was all right, and managing to cope with the training they'd be giving him.

★ ★ ★

Tansy was determined to make the most of her opportunity. No excess make-up this time, and she had borrowed an old pair of wellingtons from Mrs Matthews, the better to go tramping across country.

'And mind you don't step on no sharp sticks. Boots with holes in are no use to me, but just you try getting a pair to replace them, with this war on.' By the look of them a few sticks had been trodden on before, for the rubber was decorated by the sort of patches used in mending punctured bicycle tubes. Still, Tansy promised to do her best.

The trees dripped with moisture as she and Peter strolled through the woods, with the old dog, Ben, racing ahead of them. She felt contented as she listened to his talk of the things he'd done with his brothers before the war; tennis parties and gymkhanas, and moonlight bathes in the river. It was all far removed from the back streets of Coventry.

'I'm monopolising the conversation,' Peter said at last. 'Tell me about yourself, Tansy.'

'There's not much to tell, really.' She gave him an edited version of her past life and he seemed satisfied.

'I've enjoyed our chat,' he told her,

when they emerged from the wood. 'We must do this again soon, if I don't get my marching orders.'

'That would be lovely, Peter. I'll look forward to it.'

When Tansy reached her lodgings her landlady greeted her with a grimmer than usual expression on her already unlovely face.

'Here! This wire come while you were out. I hope it's not bad news.'

But what else could it be, Tansy fretted. Telegrams in wartime meant only one thing — trouble.

'Well, aren't you going to open it? The boy wanted to know if there was any reply, but how did I know? I didn't like to open it, see.'

'Thank you, Mrs Matthews,' Tansy replied. 'I'd like to open it on my own, if you don't mind.'

7

At the first house they reached, and then the second, nobody was at home. 'This is a great start,' Dinah observed.

'Never you mind, we can come back again later,' Emo said.

Dinah felt a warm glow at his words. Even though their outing was strictly business, she was delighted that she'd be seeing him again. Perhaps when he got to know her better, the handsome Welshman would take a liking to her, and who knew where that might lead?

'Who is this, then?' The woman who opened the door at the next house regarded Dinah with a quizzical expression.

'This is Miss Smith, Marged.'

'Oh, there's disappointing — I thought you had a new girlfriend, boyo!'

Please, please don't laugh at that, Dinah begged silently, but Emo didn't rise to the bait.

'We're here about the children from the English school,' he explained. 'You have an evacuee, don't you?'

'Oh, aye. He hasn't been complaining about me, I hope.'

'Na, na. Can we come in, Marged or do you intend to keep us standing on the doorstep?'

'Of course. Where are my manners? It took me by surprise, see, you coming here with a young lady. I thought at first it was Glynis Jones, but then I suppose she's gone for good, eh? Never mind. More fish in the sea, and all that.'

'I'll let Miss Smith tell you why we've come,' Emo said, adroitly cutting off the flow.

Dinah was intrigued. Who was this Glynis Jones, and why didn't Emo want to talk about her? More importantly, was she important in his life, and was she likely to pop up again, destroying all Dinah's hopes?

'We want to make sure that all the children get something for Christmas,' Dinah explained to Marged. 'Things in

Coventry are all at sixes and sevens and we're not sure if everyone will be able to send presents. It would be terrible if the little ones woke up to an empty stocking. Some of them are already afraid that Father Christmas won't know where they are now.'

'I hope you don't think I can do anything about that, Miss Smith. The allowance I get for keeping the boy barely covers his food. There'd be nothing left over for football boots and toy soldiers!'

'Come, now, Marged, I'm sure you can manage a packet of bull's eyes,' Emo said. 'But that's not why we've come, is it, Dinah?'

'No. We just want you to let us know if, and when, anything arrives for Donald in the post. For goodness' sake don't let him open it. Just hide it away somewhere and put it on the end of his bed after he goes to sleep on Christmas Eve. Take the outside wrapping off first, of course.'

'I don't have time to go all the way

up the school, see.'

'Then perhaps you could send a note with Donald?' Dinah suggested.

'All right, then, see. Now, if there's nothing else . . . ?'

'Whew! That was tricky,' Dinah said, when they were well out of earshot 'I'm so glad you were there. I don't know what I'd have done without you.'

'Oh, you don't want to mind what Marged says. She's a good sort, really. Known her all my life, see. I sat behind her at school and dipped her plaits in the inkwell. She's never let me forget that.'

'I should think not!' Dinah laughed at the thought. 'Where to next?'

★ ★ ★

At last they finished their rounds, having turned down numerous cups of tea and been made to promise to come again. She had made several ticks against the names on her list; obviously some of the parents were taking no chances, and had posted their gifts in plenty of time. There had been no one home at six of the houses.

'Not to worry, we can come again,' Emo said. 'Er, Miss Smith . . . Dinah . . . our mam would like to meet you, see. She's invited you to tea on Sunday. Shall I tell her you'll be there?'

'I'd love to come. Tell her thank you very much, will you? And shall I let the others know?' Dinah didn't want to make assumptions.

'What others?'

'Mrs Ramsey and Tansy.'

'Na, na, they're not invited, see. Just you.'

'Oh, sorry. People have been giving us 'welcome to Bryncollen' teas. I thought that's what this was.' Dinah tried to still her hammering heart.

'Na; na, it's you that Mam wants to meet, see,' he stressed, smiling.

'You've mentioned me to her, then?'

'Well, Auntie Gwlad has, anyway. Well, I'd better be going, then.'

Dinah didn't know what to think as

she stood watching him as he strode off jauntily, swinging his arms.

* * *

'How did it go?' Dinah's landlady asked, when she was back in the warmth of the little house.

'All right. Your sister has asked me to tea on Sunday, Emlyn says.'

'There's nice. I know she'd be glad to see him set up with a nice girl. You do like the boy, don't you? I can tell by the way he looks at you that he's taken a shine to you, see.'

'Of course I like him; he's very nice,' Dinah said, blushing.

'More than nice, I hope! Only you'll be careful not to tread on his feelings, won't you, cariad? He doesn't deserve to have his heart broken again, see.'

'Is that Glynis Jones you're talking about?'

'How do you know about her?'

'One of the women we called on today mentioned her. A Marged somebody,' Dinah replied.

'Oh, Marged Jenkins! A real gossip, that one. Best to steer clear of her, unless you want the whole town knowing your business.' Gwladys gave Dinah a friendly wink then took a deep breath. 'Well, that Glynis . . . Our Emo was going with her for a long time. Expecting to hear of an engagement any day, we all were, he was that smitten. Then he got a touch of TB and was sent off to the sanitorium, see.'

'And she finished with him then?' Dinah was horrified.

'Worse than that, cariad. She took up with another chap behind his back, a sales rep who used to call at the chemist's where she worked. The next thing we all knew, she'd eloped with him, see, gone to Swansea to be married. She didn't even tell Emo to his face, mind you, just sent him a note, like. Didn't even say sorry. Of course, his heart was broken, poor boyo, and I don't think he's trusted a girl since.'

Dinah digested all this with mixed feelings. She was sorry to think that

Emo had been hurt, yet glad to discover that he was a free agent.

But could he ever learn to trust again, though? Only time would tell.

★ ★ ★

Bronwen Rees was a shorter, plumper version of her sister. She welcomed Dinah enthusiastically, shaking her by the hand until the girl thought that her arm would drop off.

'There's lovely to see you,' she said. 'Our Gwlad has told me all about you, see. How are you liking Bryncollen?'

'Very well, thank you.'

'That's right. Come you to the fire now and warm yourself. I'll call you to the table in a minute. I'm just waiting for the tatws to boil.'

The red brick fireplace took up most of one wall of the kitchen. A coal fire burned in the grate and two steaming pots stood on the hob. By the aroma that came from them, Dinah assumed that tatws was the Welsh word for potatoes. A black oven was let into the wall beside the fire, and Mrs Rees opened this to reveal a large pie with a golden crust, which she carried to the table, set for three.

'You ask the blessing, boyo,' she said when they were seated. Heads were bowed and Emo did as he was asked, and said grace in Welsh. What a musical language Welsh was, Dinah thought.

'Now then my girl, tell us all about yourself,' Bronwen ordered, when their plates were full. 'Come from a big family, do you?'

'Don't be nosy, Mam!' Emo spluttered.

'Don't speak with your mouth full, boyo. I was speaking to Miss Smith, see. You've nothing to hide, do you, bach?'

'Please call me Dinah. And it's all right, Emlyn. There are just three of us, Mrs Rees. Mum, myself and my sister, Joyce. Dad was wounded in the last war and he never really recovered. He died when I was very young and Joyce was just a baby.'

'There's sad for your poor mam, having to bring up little ones all alone. I'm a widow too, but at least I had my man by me for longer than your mam did. Five of a family, I have, and I don't know how I could have managed if he'd gone sooner.'

'Are your other children nearby?'

'The girls are married, and not too far away. The boys are in the next valley, working down the pit, see. I'm lucky to have our Emo here. That's one good thing about him having been bad — there's no mining for him.'

Bad? What on earth had he been up to? Emo saw her horrified expression and guessed what she was thinking. 'When the Welsh speak about someone being bad, see, that's what you English would call being ill,' he explained, grinning at her.

'Oh, that's all right, then,' she said, feeling foolish.

8

Tansy was clearly distraught. 'I have to go home!' she cried. 'Back to Coventry, I mean. I'll go as soon as I can get a train!'

Dora stared at her in amazement. 'Do calm down, Miss Smith. What on earth has happened? Is your landlady being difficult or something?'

'It's my grandmother — she's dead! She's been in hospital ever since that air raid, and now she's dead!'

'I'm so sorry, dear.' Dora didn't know what to say.

'I have to be at the funeral, Mrs Ramsey. You do see that, don't you?'

'Of course you must be at the funeral. Do you know any details yet?'

Tansy pulled out the telegram from from her pocket. 'This is all it says. *Gran dead, stop. Funeral Friday, stop.*'

'And it doesn't tell you when, or where?'

'I'm sure they couldn't afford to send a longer message, but I'll find out when I get there. I expect it will be in her church, the one she always attended. Trouble is, I won't know where to go when I get there, now they've been bombed out of our house.' Tansy began to rock back and forth, as if in unspeakable pain.

'Never mind,' Dora said. 'There's an answer to this if we plan carefully. I've got a train timetable in my bag, so the first thing to do is find out when you'll be leaving here and what time you'll get in to Coventry. Not that one can be sure of anything, nowadays. There always seem to be delays on the line. Then we'll wire your parents so you can be met at the station.'

'But the boy won't know where to deliver it!' Tansy wailed. 'There's nothing left of our street. You said so yourself.'

'Address it to the vicar at your Gran's

church,' Dinah suggested. 'Your parents must be in touch with him over the funeral arrangements.'

'That sounds sensible,' Dora said. 'What about your brothers and sisters, Tansy? Will they be able to attend?'

'Don't ask me. Two of the boys are in the Navy. I suppose they might get compassionate leave but who knows where they are now? They may be in the middle of the Atlantic, for all I know.'

'Oh, well, you'll find out when you get there,' Dora told her. Privately, she wondered if anyone was getting compassionate leave nowadays. With so much bombing going on, there would hardly be anyone left in the forces if everyone was able to go home when tragedy struck.

'That's that, then,' Tansy sniffed, dabbing at her eyes with a grubby handkerchief. 'I'll be back as soon as I can, Mrs Ramsey. Would you like me to go and see your mum while I'm in Coventry, Dinah?'

'Oh, would you? I haven't had a letter this week and I want to know what's going on at home. The last time she wrote she was worried about my sister, who hadn't been heard from since the raid.'

'I expect she's back by now, safe and sound,' Dora said, 'but it will be a relief to know the full story.'

★ ★ ★

Tansy arrived in Coventry, exhausted from the journey. The train out of London had been late, and she'd had to stand all the way, crushed by a mass of passengers who, like herself, had been unable to obtain seats.

'I don't know what the world is coming to,' the woman standing next to her grumbled. 'No manners at all. There was a time when a man would get up and offer his seat to a lady, but no more.'

Tansy was too tired to respond. When they finally reached Coventry she almost fell off the train, and was grateful when a passing porter — an elderly man — caught her by the arm.

'Steady on, love. You almost lost your balance there. I thought you was sleep-walking, the way you was going.'

Tansy thanked him and staggered down the platform, oblivious to the people she bumped into. At the exit she looked in vain for a familiar face but there was nobody there to meet her. With a sigh she looked around for a bus, and when one came lurching around the corner she heaved herself on, grateful to find an empty seat.

A cheerful clippie asked her where she was going and for a long moment she had to think. At last she named the church and was given a ticket and a few coppers' worth of change.

'I'll let you know when we get there, in case you fall asleep,' the girl said. 'You look all in. I suppose you didn't get any sleep on the train?'

'Not much chance of that, standing in the corridor.'

'No, I s'pose not.' The clippie moved on, humming a few bars of some popular song. How could she be so cheerful when their once beautiful city lay in ruins all around them? Tansy supposed that it was all part of showing Hitler that the British could not be beaten.

She found the harrassed vicar in the church, coming down from the pulpit, where he had been arranging papers.

'Excuse me, is there to be a funeral here today?'

'Yes. Mrs Marsden, is it, or Miss Sparks?'

'No, Mrs Smith.'

'Yes, that's right, but you're early, I'm afraid. You'll have to come back at two o'clock. I've a baptism here in half an hour and I'm afraid I've no time to stop and chat.'

Tansy sank down in the nearest pew. 'I don't suppose you know where the Smiths are living at the moment? I've just come from Wales, you see. I've been travelling all night and I don't know where to go next. My family were bombed out recently and I've no idea where they are.'

'I'm afraid I don't know, either, but you I can do something about. Just come with me and my wife will find you something to eat and make you a nice hot cup of tea. Things always look a bit better after a cup of tea, I always think.'

Tansy doubted that anything could improve her spirits right at that moment, but it was true; after swallowing a scalding brew that almost burned her tongue, she did feel somewhat revived.

'Thank you so very much,' she told the vicar's wife, who was hovering about with a duster in her hand. 'I'll be going now. I mustn't hold you up when you're busy.'

'Nonsense. You can't go wandering aimlessly about, waiting for two o'clock! You can lie down on the settee and have a little nap. When your parents arrive, Richard will let them know you're here.'

'Well if you're sure . . . ' Tansy

removed her coat and shoes and curled up on the sagging settee. The last thing she remembered was the lady of the house arranging a worn blanket over her, and then she sank into a dreamless sleep. After what seemed like a very short time she was woken by a kiss on her forehead, and there was Mum.

'There you are, love! We didn't know if you'd get here.'

'I sent a wire,' Tansy said groggily.

'I'm sure you did, but we never had it. Never mind, you're here now.'

To Tansy's dismay there were three coffins lined up in the aisle. Her mum explained that with so many people dead and dying, nothing was normal any more. The poor vicar couldn't spend twenty-four hours a day conducting one service after another. He had to double up on a good many of them. Tansy reflected that he must have been glad to have a christening that morning, welcoming a new, innocent life into the church after all that carnage.

Poor old Gran! In her latter years

she'd talked a lot about the good send-off she'd intended to have. She'd been salting away money at the post office to pay for it all. Now she had to share her final departure with two women who were completely unknown to her.

Later, there was a brief family reunion in a chip shop; hardly a very classy affair. Tansy had been to other funerals in her day, when a nice ham dinner was served. However, as Dad explained, this was their best bet because unlike other food, fish and chips was not rationed when served in a place like this. And it wasn't as if anybody from outside the family was with them, so there was no need to keep up appearances.

Somehow the smell of vinegar and grease was comforting. Perhaps Gran would have approved.

'You'll have to tell me where you're all living,' Tansy said, when the last delicious morsel had disappeared. 'I promised to go and see my friend's mother, and I'll need to know where to find you later on.'

'Oh, love! We're scattered about all over the place! Your dad and I have spent the last few nights on a mattress on the floor of the church hall. You can't even come there, for there's not an inch to spare. I'm afraid you may have to ask your friend's mother to put you up, love. I'm sure she won't mind. I'd do the same for her girl, in other circumstances.'

★　★　★

The door was flung open so quickly that Tansy was taken by surprise. She scarcely recognised the distraught woman in front of her, although she had met Dinah's mother in the past at school functions.

'Where on earth have you been, you naughty girl? Don't you know I've been half out of mind with worry?'

'Mrs Blake? Do you remember me?' she said gently. 'I'm Tansy Smith, a colleague of Dinah's.'

'Oh, of course you are. I'm so sorry. Do come in. I'm afraid I hoped you were my other daughter, Joyce. She's been missing for days.'

Tansy followed as Mrs Blake led the way into the kitchen. It was a cheerless place, with piles of unwashed crockery in the sink, and a coat thrown across the back of a chair. Despite the time of day the blackout curtains were not yet drawn across the windows, yet the dim light from one small bulb did little to dispel the general gloom.

'Do sit down, Miss Smith. Perhaps you'd like a cup of tea?' Mrs Blake flustered. 'That's if I can find the tea caddy. I can't think where I've put it, but it must be here somewhere.'

Tansy's heart went out to the woman. 'Let me put the kettle on, Mrs Blake. Have you eaten today yet?'

'I can't remember . . . '

'I'll make you a bit of toast then, shall I? And do you mind if I put the blackout down? You don't want the warden to see a light showing and give you a fine.'

'Do as you please, for all the good it's done us. They found poor old Coventry, didn't they, those bombers? Even without a chink of light showing. Still, please yourself. I suppose you're not used to the blackout, are you, down in Wales?'

'Dinah wanted me to call to see how you are, Mrs Blake. She's been very worried about you. Your last letter upset her a bit, you see. First she thought you were safe in Leamington, and then . . . '

'Then I came home and found our Joyce missing.'

'I'm sure that was terribly upsetting for you.'

'You can't possibly know how I felt.'

'I'm afraid I have a pretty good idea, Mrs Blake. I've just come from my gran's funeral. She was at home when our house was bombed, and she was trapped under the rubble for almost two days before they brought her out. She was taken to hospital, but they couldn't save her. It was a heart attack, they told Mum, brought on by the shock.'

'I'm so sorry,' Mrs Blake murmured, shame-faced.

'Why don't you tell me about Joyce?' Tansy asked gently

'Well, after we heard about the raid I was worried about her, being all alone here. Mother was feeling a bit better and she quite understood why I had to leave earlier than I'd promised. Joyce wasn't here when I came home, but I wasn't worried at first. She works shifts, you see, and naturally I thought she must be at work.'

'She's on the buses, isn't she?' Tansy asked.

'That's right. When she wasn't home by supper time I was starting to get concerned, but even then I assumed she was all right. She wasn't expecting me back, you see, so I thought she was out with friends, or staying overnight with another girl. But when morning came and she still hadn't put in an appearance I went down to the depot to ask about her. The manager was a bit nasty. Said she hadn't turned up for work two days in a row, and if it wasn't for the fact there's a war on he'd give her the sack. He'd had to bring someone back from her days off to take Tansy's place, and there had been unpleasantness all round.'

'Oh, dear.' Tansy patted the older woman's hand synpathetically.

'Well, I wasn't having that! I told him straight, I said 'There's no need to take that tone with me, my man! My daughter has gone missing, and for all you know she could be lying dead somewhere, unidentified.' That shook him up a bit and he apologised, but what good was that? It brought me no nearer to finding out what had happened to her.'

'No, indeed.'

'After that I checked with all her friends, everyone I could think of, but nobody could tell me anything. I tried the hospitals, the relief centres, the Red

Cross, the Home Guard, you name it. It seems as if Joyce has just vanished off the face of the earth.'

'I'm so sorry. If there's anything I can do . . .'

'You can tell Dinah she's to let me know at once if she hears from her,' she said distractedly.

'I'll certainly do that.' Tansy didn't know what else to say. 'I'd better be going, Mrs Blake. I have to find somewhere to spend the night before it gets too dark, because there isn't a train back to London until morning.'

This was Mrs Blake's cue to offer Tansy a bed, but the remark didn't seem to register. 'I'll show you out, then, dear. Thank you so much for coming. Give my love to Dinah when you see her.'

Tansy set off for the station, her thoughts veering back and forth between sympathy for the woman and resentment. It wouldn't have hurt Mrs Blake to let her sleep in Dinah's room. Perhaps she should have asked outright, but that would have seemed rude, especially when she didn't know the woman all that well.

She knew that her chances of finding a place to stay were practically nil and in any case she couldn't afford a hotel. She would have to spend the night sitting on a hard wooden bench on a station platform. That was if she was lucky enough to find one that wasn't already occupied.

* * *

By the time Tansy returned to Bryncollen, after two changes of train, she had made up her mind. Without even stopping at her own lodgings she called on Dora.

'Oh, hello! You're back, then. Do come inside where it's warm. You look all in. I'll ask Mrs Llewellyn if she'll make us a cup of tea. You look as though you could do with something stronger, but this is a teetotal house. They've signed the Pledge.'

'I'm handing in my notice, Mrs

Ramsey. Don't try to talk me out of it. I've made up my mind. I'm going to join the WAAFs.'

'What on earth brought this on?'

'You've seen what they did to poor Coventry, and I'm sure that's not the only place that's going to get it before this war is over. They killed my poor gran, Mrs Ramsey, and I'm not letting them get away with it.'

'I'm sure we all feel like that, dear, but have you thought this through? You're a woman. It's not as if you can go up in a plane and drop bombs on Germany, is it? They'll have you doing secretarial work, or cooking for the men. All useful to the war effort, no doubt, but hardly the same thing.'

'I must do something to pay them back.'

'If that's the way you feel, wouldn't you be more use in a factory, making munitions, or parts for aircraft?' But Dora could see that there was no use in arguing the toss. Years of dealing with uncooperative children had given her a certain low cunning in such matters. 'We'll discuss this another time, Miss Smith. For now, you are to go to your bed and get a good night's sleep. If you don't feel up to coming to school first thing, then indulge yourself with a nice lie-in. Miss Blake and I will manage. Ah, here comes our tea. Drink up and buck up, that's what I always say.'

As Dora had hoped, Tansy did not come to school in the morning. Sleep was what the poor girl needed, and sleep she should have.

'Isn't she coming in?' Dinah wanted to know.

'Perhaps later. She had a beast of a journey there and back, and if she doesn't sleep it off she'll collapse, and we certainly don't want that. We can manage the classes between us, can't we?'

'Of course, but I wanted to ask if she found the time to call on Mum.'

'I gather that she did. She didn't say much, only that your mother hasn't heard from your sister yet.'

'Oh, no! Poor Mum! Poor Joyce! What if anything's happened to her.'

'There may be a perfectly simple explanation, you know.'

'And what might that be? She's been roped in as a spy, and sent over to France, perhaps?'

Dora smiled. 'Now you're being silly. Go and ring the bell, will you? We're five minutes late already.'

She smiled sadly at her young colleague's retreating back. She would never say so to Dinah, but she was convinced that poor Joyce was among the hundreds who had been killed in Coventry. The damage to buildings had been so bad that there were probably more people whose bodies had not yet been recovered. For the family's sake she hoped that if Joyce was dead, her remains would be found soon. There was nothing worse than not knowing what had become of someone you loved. You couldn't mourn properly while hope remained.

Meanwhile, she hoped that Tansy

could be persuaded to change her mind. If the time came when Dinah, too, had to return home for a loved one's funeral, Dora couldn't manage the whole school on her own. The pupils were unsettled enough as it was.

9

The outing was not going well at all. Emlyn and Dinah were walking down a narrow road with hedges on both sides. The morning was crisp and clear, and the trees were sparkling with frost. Normally she enjoyed a country walk, and there was much of Bryncollen she wasn't familiar with yet. Still, she wished there was something else they could do. There was nothing good on at the pictures, and she had already been to tea with Emo's mother.

The difficulty was that she couldn't think of anything to say to Emo. How she wished she could be like Tansy, who always had a good line of chat. Unfortunately she had always been quiet, only coming out with a remark when she had something to say.

A girl with a similar problem had written to the agony aunt in a popular magazine for women. 'Ask him about his work,' was the suggestion offered. 'A man always likes a girl who takes an interest in him.' But Dinah had already exhausted that subject.

Emo was also quiet, too, which wasn't like him. She hoped she hadn't offended him in some way.

Suddenly he spoke up. 'Is there anything wrong, Dinah?' He looked so concerned that she broke into tears.

'Everything is so awful! I know I shouldn't complain when so many poor souls have it worse than me, but I can't help it. My sister is still missing and now Tansy is thinking of giving up teaching and going to join up. And I know that the children are missing their parents and worried about what could happen to them. It shows in their school work. It almost seems wrong to be safe here in Bryncollen when I think of what happened at home.'

'Take this and mop up,' Emo said gently, handing her a handkerchief. She took it and dabbed at her eyes, although the tears kept coming.

'The little ones keep asking me if the bombs will start coming here and I tell them no, but what if I'm lying to them, Emlyn? How do we know what will happen next?'

'Of course you're not lying, cariad. Why should the Luftwaffe take an interest in Bryncollen? No targets here, see. No factories or dockyards.'

Dinah's heart leapt. He had called her 'cariad', which she now knew was a Welsh form of darling. Then she told herself to calm down. It was just a figure of speech. Gwladys Richards used it on a regular basis, just as the English might say dear, or love. She had read that people in the acting profession addressed each other as darling on a regular basis. No, Emo was just being kind.

'I'm so sorry, I've been moaning on about myself, when you seem worried too. Is there something on your mind?'

'Swansea,' he said. 'I've got to go to Swansea, see.'

'You're not moving there to live, are you?' she asked, alarmed.

'Na, na. Just a quick trip to the big hospital there, to get an x-ray,' he told her. 'I have to go once a year, just for a check-up on my lungs.'

'That won't be too bad, will it? I mean, x-rays don't hurt, do they?' Never having had one, Dinah wasn't sure what was involved.

'There's nothing to it. In and out in minutes, you are. It's going to Swansea itself that bothers me. They've had terrible bombing too, on account of the docks, see, months before Coventry was hit. Feelings are running high down there and I don't like the thought of walking through the streets in civvies when every other man in sight is in uniform.'

Dinah considered this for a moment. She had heard her mother say that during the last war, women had given white feathers to any man they spotted who was not in uniform. Surely that custom had died out now? And why should anyone assume that a man in civilian dress was a coward, or an enemy sympathiser? He might have been rejected for health reasons, like Emo, or engaged in vital war work which gave him exemption; a coal miner, say, or a farmer.

'Would you have joined up if you hadn't had the problem with your lungs?' she asked him.

'I tried to enlist, Dinah. As soon as it came to the medical I was out on my ear. Tried at three different recruiting offices, I did, until the last doctor I saw told me to go home and find outdoor work. So, here I am.'

'You've nothing to be ashamed of, Emlyn. You've taken the place of the previous gamekeeper, who's gone to join the Army. That's worth something, surely?'

'All right round here, where they all know me, but it's a different story if I leave home, like. Do you think I want to be called a conchie?'

Dinah knew that a conscientious

163

objector was someone who refused to kill because of his religious or moral beliefs. Such men were called up before a tribunal, hoping to be given exemption from service. Very often they were sent to work on the land, or sent to the front lines with the Army, to work as stretcher bearers, which was a highly dangerous job.

'But if people really believe it's wrong to kill . . . ' she began.

'Some do, and some don't, Dinah. Besides, you've got to think of the bigger picture, see. Hitler is planning to invade us. We can't just let him walk in and take over, can we? I for one will be ready, armed with my shotgun and pitchfork.' He smiled briefly, but Dinah could see that he meant what he said.

'Yes, well, before that you've got to go to Swansea. I tell you what; if you like I'll come with you when you go?'

'Come with me? But how can you get away from your teaching?'

'It's the school holidays, isn't it? The children don't really need us, and if anything does crop up they can go to Mrs Ramsey.'

'Well, if you're sure you want to . . .'

'I can have a look round the shops while you're at the hospital. There might even be sales on after Christmas — if there's anything left to buy.'

'And if the cinemas are open we could go to the pictures. Swansea always gets the new films long before they come to Bryncollen.'

So here she was, about to have a real date at last! Dinah could hardly believe that she had invited herself, but Emo didn't seem to mind. Feeling cheerful, she said goodbye to her handsome Welshman and returned to her lodgings, where she settled down to address the few Christmas cards she had bought.

* * *

When they arrived in Swansea, early in the New Year, she almost wished she hadn't come. There was so much

165

devastation. The people seemed cheerful enough, obviously determined not to give in, despite what might be thrown at them by the enemy from across the Channel. But oh, the sight of the ruined houses and shops!

Dinah stared up at one house which had the whole front sheared off. Amazingly, some bits of furniture still remained in the rooms, and a picture hung askew on a bedroom wall.

It reminded her of the doll's house she had shared with Joyce when they were young; the front opened on hinges so you could arrange everything inside.

By afternoon, Emo had joined her in the tea shop where they'd agreed beforehand to meet up.

'Did you get the all-clear?'

'They'll let me know later. The films have to be read by a specialist, and he wasn't there today. I'm starving — what have they got to eat?'

'Beans on toast?'

'There's lovely. I like a good bean, I

do. And a strong cup of sweet tea is what I need, after walking all the way back from the hospital.'

'I hope you've brought your own sugar with you, then,' the waitress told him. 'There's a war on, in case you haven't noticed.'

Later, in the darkened cinema, Emo put his arm round Dinah's shoulders, and after a moment of indecision she snuggled as close to him as the arm of the seat next to her would allow. The second feature was showing when they came in but having missed the beginning she wasn't sure what it was all about. The story, seen in grainy black and white, seemed to be set in Ireland, where several women with shawls over their heads, were seated beside a coffin, keening mournfully.

Then came the news; all to do with the war, of course, featuring bracing bits and pieces about the Allies' pitifully few advances.

After that the main picture, *Road to Singapore*, starring Bob Hope, Dorothy

Lamour and Bing Crosby. Unfortunately they had to come out before the end because they couldn't risk missing the last train.

Many things had changed because there was a war on, but a school teacher still had to think about her reputation. Spending a night away from home in the company of a young man was definitely unacceptable.

The waiting room was packed when they arrived at the station, and there was a long queue at the refreshment counter. Having seen the rather nasty-looking sandwiches on offer Dinah decided that she could do without something more to eat. 'And I don't much like the look of that tea, either,' she remarked. 'It's bright orange!'

'It's too hot in here anyway,' Emo answered. 'The train should be here soon. Let's wait outside, shall we?'

On the darkened platform he took her into his arms and kissed her lightly on the cheek. She looked up at him, unresisting. He kissed her again, on the lips this time, a sweet, lingering sensation that made her senses reel. This was nothing like the occasional clumsy kiss she'd received as a teen-ager.

'I think I'm falling in love with you, cariad,' he said softly.

Her whispered reply was lost in the the whistle of their train.

10

Dora Ramsey felt particularly happy, all things considered. This January day in 1941 had brought several good things, the best being three letters from her husband.

'I've been so worried, not hearing from him in weeks,' she told her landlady, Sian Llewellyn. 'I've been imagining all sorts of things, but according to these letters he's still in England getting on with his training.'

'Ah, the post is all mixed up, I expect, what with bombing all over the place. Does he say anything interesting, like?'

'Not really. Just a lot of moans about spit and polish and route marches, whatever they are. Still, I'm glad to know he's all right. He didn't have to go, you know; not at his age. I wanted him to stay, but he wouldn't have it.'

'Just as well, love. If he'd stayed in Coventry, who knows what could have happened to him? And you'd be apart anyway, you being evacuated with the children.'

'I suppose you're right.'

'And what about Miss Smith? Has she made up her mind what to do?'

'I'm glad to say she's agreed to stay here until the end of the school year. Then she'll look around, as she puts it. Mind you, with any luck at all this wretched war should be over by then, and we'll all be able to get back to normal.'

'Thank goodness she's come to her senses, then,' Sian said. 'There's terrible it would be to leave you short-handed and only Miss Blake to help you out with all those children.'

'Miss Blake is very good with the young ones, but I can't deny we'd be in difficulty with only the two of us. I must admit I felt awful giving Miss Smith such a talking-to over it all, when she's had such a sad time, but as I told her, there is a war on. We must all do our duty, come what may.'

Sian chuckled. 'Was it her duty she was thinking of when she decided to stay in Bryncollen — or a certain young man?'

'Oh, tell me it's not Emlyn Rees!'

'Nothing wrong with Emo, is there? Anyway, I hear tell that he's other fish to fry,' Sian said with a wink.

'I didn't mean that. It's just that young Dinah seems to have her heart set on him, and I've been hoping he feels the same.'

'That's what I meant, love. A little bird tells me he's quite smitten. Did you know they had a day trip to Swansea last week?'

'She did hint at something of the sort. But if he's not Miss Smith's light of love, then who is?' Dora persisted.

'Young Williams, up at the big house.'

'Which one?'

'Ah, now that would be telling!'

'Come on, Mrs Llewellyn, spill the beans! You know I'd keep what you tell me in strictest confidence.'

'It's a bit late for that, with everyone at the chapel talking about it. She's been seen walking out with two of them, if not all three!'

'Which ones? Surely not Paul, the eldest? I've met him once or twice; a bit of a stuffed shirt, I thought,' Dora confessed.

'He has a right to be a bit uppity, considering he's to inherit that great estate when his da goes. Of course, he has to come through the war first, but Mrs Williams is not about to let her son and heir marry a little school teacher — and English, at that.'

Seeing the pinched look on Dora's face, she hastily amended her words. 'I didn't mean to imply there's anything wrong with being a teacher, love. The Welsh have a great respect for people with learning. It's always been considered a wonderful thing if a child grows up to become a minister or a teacher. Aye, but Paul Williams will have to marry one of his own sort, one of those hunting ladies who've been to finishing school, don't you see? He'll have a position to keep up.'

'But the other two? Won't they be free to make their own choices, when it comes to taking a wife?'

'That all depends on whether Mr Paul survives. If anything happens to him, I suppose Mr Peter will step into his shoes. As for that Philip, she'd be wise to steer clear of him. Spoiled, he is, and selfish with it. You tell her from me that if she wants her heart broken she's going the right way about it if she messes with him.'

'As far as I know he's already left Bryncollen.'

'Not to worry, then,' Sian said as if that were that.

★ ★ ★

Tansy, meanwhile, had decided for herself that Philip Williams was a lost cause. It had been all right at first, a giddy flirtation with a few stolen kisses, but he was not husband material. At least, not where she was concerned. Any woman who was unlucky enough to marry him would never have a moment's peace, wondering what he was up to. Tansy was not the sort of person to sit meekly at home while her man showed other women a good time.

On the other hand, the more she came to know Peter, the more she liked him. He had a lively sense of humour, and he liked to discuss his favourite books with her, which made her feel important. She went to the library and took out some of the titles he recommended, and if some of them were a bit heavy going, so what? She believed that reading them provided her with clues to his character, and that was all to the good.

On this January morning she had collected the latest offerings and was walking towards Dora's lodgings, wondering whether to stop in to discuss the forthcoming school concert. That was when she noticed a young woman — a

175

girl, really — loitering near the gate. She was wearing a smart red wool jacket and matching beret, and navy-blue trousers!

Women often wore trousers now, particularly those who worked in factories, and these garments were both warm and practical. In Bryncollen, though, they were considered 'fast'. Tansy would have liked to wear them herself but she knew that the school governors would have something to say if she did, and 'wearing man's clothing' would be the least of it.

'Excuse me!' The girl called out to Tansy as she approached. 'Can you tell me if this is where the Ramseys live?'

'Mrs Ramsey lodges here, yes.'

'Not Mr Ramsey?'

'I don't think so.' What an odd question. Tansy hurried past before the stranger could ply her with any more requests. She wasn't about to divulge any of the Head's private business to this girl, whoever she was. Let her knock on the door and speak to Mrs

Ramsey herself, if she had legitimate business here.

Careless talk costs lives. That was one of the slogans that were being drummed into the British public nowadays. There were supposed to be enemy agents all over the place, trying to find out things which would help their cause. The girl didn't look like Tansy's idea of a spy, but then, what did spies look like? And why come to Bryncollen? There were no factories, or military installations here to be infiltrated. And what could a spy want with Jim Ramsey? He was in England, training to be a soldier.

Of course, Tansy had only Dora's word for that. What if he was doing something else entirely, secret war work of his own? She laughed at herself for being an idiot. The idea of stolid Jim Ramsey being parachuted behind enemy lines was laughable in the extreme.

She looked back, and saw that the girl was now standing at the door of Dora's lodgings. It was exasperating, not knowing what it was all about. She hoped that Dora would satisfy her curiosity later. There had to be a simple explanation.

'Somebody here to see you, Mrs Ramsey.' Looking the visitor up and down, Sian Llewellyn kept the girl waiting on the doorstep.

Dora didn't recognise her visitor. 'Yes, can I help you?'

'Can I come in? I've come all the way from Coventry.'

'Of course. Come this way, please.' Behind them, Sian shut the front door with a bang. That was another black mark against the girl. In Bryncollen people always came to the back. The front door was for weddings and funerals.

'It's really Mr Ramsey I've come to see,' the girl began, when she and Dora were sitting in the front parlour. Outside the door, Sian strained her ears to try to hear what was being said. If she could only open it a crack it would be a help, but that door was inclined to squeak. She reminded herself to oil the hinges before the day was out.

Dora's eyebrows disappeared into her curls. 'I don't know what made you think you'd find him here, Miss, er . . . ?'

'Oattes. Paisley Oattes.'

'My husband is away, serving in the Army. If you'd taken the trouble to write to me first, you could have saved yourself a wasted journey.'

'They said you'd all been evacuated to Wales.'

'I don't know who 'they' are, but they were only half right. I brought the children here from our school, just a few months before the bombing. In fact, my first thought was that you were the mother of one of the infants, come to see your child.'

Paisley shook her head, frowning. Another thought struck Dora.

'I say, it's not bad news, is it? you're not here to tell us something about Joyce Blake, are you?'

'Never heard of any Joyce Blake. I

told you, it's your husband I want to see. If he's not here I need to find him right away, Mrs Ramsey. You see, James Ramsey is my father . . . '

★   ★   ★

Dora felt as if all the breath had been punched out of her. *I am not going to faint*, she told herself, feeling for a chair. The girl sat down next to her, without waiting for an invitation.

Dora willed herself to keep an impassive face. 'There must be some mistake,' she managed to say at last. 'We've never had children, I'm sad to say, so unfortunately you've come all this way for nothing. I expect you've been misdirected. Possibly your father is another man of the same name. He certainly isn't my husband.'

'But I was told that his wife used to teach at the Soper Street School, and that she's been evacuated to this Bryncollen place. That is you?'

'Well, obviously I fit that description,

but you've still got it wrong. What exactly did they tell you at the orphanage?'

'What orphanage?'

'I'm sorry. I assumed that you must have been brought up in an orphanage, if you're only now searching out your father.'

Dora knew of many sad stories where a mother had died, or become unable to cope, and her husband had been unable to take on child-rearing responsibilities. Perhaps he was a merchant seaman, or a travelling salesman, seldom in one place for long. The children were then placed in an orphanage. Worse still, many were shipped off to Canada or Australia, to begin a new life far from everything they knew and loved.

'I'm not an orphan. I've got a mother.'

'Then I think you'd better tell me what all this is about,' Dora said.

The girl took a deep breath. 'Mum was in love with this chap when she was just a teenager, see. When she told him she was expecting me he couldn't face it. He ran off, and she never heard from him again.'

Dora nodded. It was a too familiar story. 'She brought you up alone?'

'Sort of. We lived with my grandparents and I always thought my gran was my mum. My Uncle Des was only five when I was born, and everyone thought I was just the next one in line. I remember hearing her tell a neighbour she was 'caught in the change' and that's how I came.'

Again, Dora had heard such stories many a time. It was a handy solution to the problem of an unexpected pregnancy, covering it with a cloak of respectability at the same time.

'And your father didn't enter into the picture at all?'

'I said so, didn't I? Not that he was missed, because I thought Gramps was my dad, you know?'

'Then why look for him now?'

'It's the air raid on Coventry, see? My

182

grandparents are both dead, but me and Mum were still living in the same house where I was brought up. We lost everything in the bombing and now we have nowhere to go. No jobs, either. We both worked in the laundry round the corner, but that bought it as well. So Mum says to me 'you'll have to go and find your father, Paisley'. That's me, see? Paisley Oattes. 'He'll have to look after us now, and about time, too.' So I made inquiries, and here I am.'

'That's a bit much, isn't it, after all these years? How old are you?'

'I'll be nineteen come May.'

'So why didn't you try to contact this man before now?' Dora retorted.

'Mum has her pride, doesn't she? Anyway we managed all right until my grandparents died, but now our house is gone and our livelihood, too. Where are we supposed to turn?'

'I'm sorry to hear about your home. I lost everything, too, you know.'

'So did a lot of people, but you get a fat wage as a teacher, eh, and a husband to keep you as well. Some people get all the luck.'

Dora almost laughed at the notion of a teacher — and a female one at that — earning a large salary. Still, it probably was more than this girl could ever earn as a laundress.

'So,' the girl went on, 'just tell me where I can find your husband, and I'll be on my way.'

'My husband is in the Army, and I've no idea where he is at the moment.' Dora crossed her fingers inside her skirt pocket. It wasn't really a lie, she told herself. Jim could be anywhere by now. The Army was always shipping men here, there and everywhere. 'Even if I could tell you where to find him, there's no point in you going to look for him. By now he could be in Italy, or Africa or somewhere. Why go off on a wild goose chase, when I'm absolutely sure he isn't the man you want anyway?'

The girl fumbled in her handbag. 'Take a look at this, then, and you'll know I'm speaking the truth.' She handed over a postcard-sized snapshot, the type that professional photographers often snapped in holiday resorts in the hope that people would buy the finished product.

The photo, a typical holiday snapshot of four young people, appeared to have been taken on a beach, with a background of rocks. Two young men had their arms around the shoulders of two girls of similar age. It was obvious that the picture hadn't been taken recently, for the men wore black swimsuits which covered them from shoulder to thigh, with large holes cut out of the sides, and no doubt the wearers felt their costumes were the last word in sophistication.

Dora felt her stomach heave as her gaze went to the face of one of the young men. That was Jim Ramsey as he had been when she first met him; tall, skinny, and wearing a cocky grin on his face.

'That's him, see?' the girl said, stabbing a finger on the image of

Dora's husband as a young man.

'I can't say. It's too small to make him out. I'll have to find a magnifying glass to identify him properly. Leave this with me for now, and we'll talk about it later.'

'Oh, no you don't, madam!' Paisley snatched the photo away. 'And have you destroy the evidence? I wasn't born yesterday, you know! I'll come back tomorrow, and you'd better be ready to talk about my compensation, or else!' She flounced out of the house, slamming the door behind her.

'Is everything all right here? I thought I heard raised voices.' Dora's landlady entered the room, a look of concern on her homely face.

'I'm afraid it's not all right, Mrs Llewellyn. Something rather awful has cropped up, and I have no idea how I'm going to handle it.'

'Would it help if you told me about it? You know what they say, a trouble shared is a trouble halved.'

Dora's instinct told her to say

nothing, for that would be disloyal to Jim. On the other hand, if she didn't let off steam she felt she might burst, and having a stroke wouldn't help the situation.

'It's that girl,' she began.

'I thought it might be. Trouble written all over her, I thought. Begging for money, I suppose.'

'How did you know?'

'Isn't it obvious? Why else would she trouble to come all the way from Coventry to speak to a stranger if it wasn't to her advantage? That is, if she is a stranger to you?'

'She insists my husband is her father, and now she and her mother have fallen on hard times, they expect him to help them out financially.'

'Never!'

'At first I believed it was a hideous mistake, that it must be someone with a similar name, but she has an old snap of a group of people which shows my husband as a very young man.'

'That doesn't mean a thing! Who else

is in the picture? Is the girl's mother in it?'

'I don't know,' Dora confessed. 'She didn't actually say. All this has me so confused, Mrs Llewellyn. I couldn't think of the right questions.'

'I shouldn't think you could! I hope you jolly well sent her off with a flea in her ear!'

'I'm afraid I couldn't pull myself together in time to do anything. The girl says she's coming back tomorrow and I must gather my wits by then.'

'Look here, Mrs Ramsey. I don't suppose this is any of my business, really, but I can't stand by and see you taken in. I've heard of this sort of thing before. There's a big blitz somewhere, people bombed out, fires all over the place, people injured. Most people do everything they can to help. But there's the other sort, who don't care about their fellow human beings. Stealing, looting, putting up the prices of food in their shops.'

'It's to be hoped they're few and far

188

between,' Dora said sadly.

'And I prefer to believe that is the case,' her landlady replied, looking stern. 'But there's something not right about this one's story, and until you get to the bottom of it you mustn't hand over so much as a penny!'

'It all comes down to the same thing,' Dora wailed. 'Where would this girl get a picture of my Jim in his young days if her story isn't true? It's not as if I've ever heard of this Paisley Oattes, or whatever she calls herself.'

11

A rattle came at the front door letterbox, just as Dinah was hastily swallowing her last morsel of toast.

'That's Evans the Post,' Gwladys said cheerily.

'I'm late, then,' Dinah said, wiping her mouth as she stood up. 'I'll just grab my coat and then I'll have to run.'

'Nothing for me today,' her landlady said, returning with a letter in her hand, 'but here's one for you, postmarked Coventry.'

'Thanks, Mrs Richards. I'll have to read it later. I don't have time.'

'But don't you want to know what's in it? It may be from your mam, with news of your sister!' It was plain that Gwladys was eager to know what the letter contained; come to that, Dinah was desperate as well. How could she wait until playtime to read it? She ripped open the envelope, skimmed through the letter inside and gave a great gasp.

'What is it, cariad? Is it from your mam? Is it about your sister?'

'Yes, it's from Mum, and Joyce is alive and well!'

'Thank the Lord!'

Dinah thrust the letter into her pocket. 'I'll see you later, Mrs Richards. At this rate I'll be lucky to get there before the bell.'

'But your sister! Where has she been all this time?'

'I'll tell you all about it at tea time,' she called over her shoulder.

Running up the road, Dinah tried to quell the thoughts that were racing through her head. She needed time to digest this, and she knew she couldn't manage to do that while trying to help the infants with their sums. It might be as well to review their times tables with the children. That would not require too much effort on her part.

* * *

'Three ones are three. Three twos are six. Three threes are . . . '

A boy put up his hand. 'This is too hard, Miss! Why can't we do the two times? I know that one.'

'All you have to do is concentrate, Joshua. If you say it often enough it will get into your head and stick there.'

'But, Miss . . . ' Joshua gave Dinah a pathetically cute pouting look.

'Now that's enough. When you get in with the big boys, you'll have to learn tables right up to the twelve times. What do you think about that?'

A groan echoed across the classroom. Dinah could sympathise. She wasn't too sure about the eight times table herself!

'Now then, children; shall we begin again? Three ones are three . . . '

Somehow Dinah got through the day. It seemed that three-thirty would never come, but when it did she rushed out of school without even stopping to chat to her colleagues. She followed the scampering children along the lane and then, reaching a stile which gave access to a farmer's field, she sat down and read her letter again.

You'll be glad to hear that Joyce is safe, her mother had written. With a pang, Dinah noticed that the ink had smeared where tears had fallen on the page. Poor Mum! *She walked in this afternoon, bold as brass, looking very pleased with herself. But it will come as a surprise to you — a shock, I should say — that the naughty girl is married!*

As she read on, Dinah could imagine the scene as clearly as if she had been there. Mum heating up a tin of soup for herself, being too upset to cook a proper meal, then the door opened, and there was Joyce.

'Joyce! Oh, Joyce! You're alive!'

'Of course I'm alive, Mum!'

'But where have you been? I thought

you were dead! I've been to the bus depot, I've visited the hospitals, I've asked everyone I can think of if they've seen you. It was as if you'd vanished off the face of the earth.'

'Didn't you get my postcards?'

'What postcards?'

'I sent you one every day from Whitley Bay.'

'Whitley Bay? What on earth were you doing there?'

'I was on my honeymoon. I'm married, Mum!' Joyce held out her left hand to display a narrow gold band on her third finger.

'Married! But I didn't even know you were seeing anybody special. Oh, dear, I've got to sit down. I've come over all queer!'

★ ★ ★

'And that's all I know,' Dinah told Gwladys over the tea table. 'She's alive, and she's married.'

'There's romantic, cariad! But who is

the chap? Has she been seeing him long, do you know?'

'Your guess is as good as mine, Mrs Richards. Mum thought I'd want to know as soon as possible that Joyce is safe, and she wanted to rush down to the pillar box to catch the last collection. When she reached the foot of the page she signed off, saying 'more later'. We'll just have to wait for the next instalment.'

The back door opened and Emlyn appeared. His aunt greeted him, bright-eyed. 'We've had good news, boyo! Dinah's sister has turned up, see, just like the prodigal son in the Scriptures.'

'And has your mam killed the fatted calf for her?' Emo asked, with an amused smile.

Dinah pulled a face. 'I don't know about that! Of course Mum is thrilled that Joyce is all right, but I'm not so sure how she feels about the fact that she's got married.'

'Married?'

'It seems so, but Mum knew nothing

about it until Joyce turned up again,' Dinah explained.

'How could that be? Did they elope, or what?' Emo asked.

'I gather it happened while Mum was in Leamington, but so far we don't know who the lucky man is.'

Emo frowned. 'They must do things differently in England, then. In Bryn-collen it always goes the same way. First a couple go walking out for a bit, and then the chap takes the girl home to meet the family. If his mam approves, the next step is going to tea with her family, for the girl's da to give the boy the once-over. Then it's official, see, and they start attending chapel together, like.'

'You mean they're engaged then?'

'Na, na. That has to wait until they've saved up a bit of money. It doesn't do to start married life with nothing in your stocking.'

'I've known some who have done that,' his aunt said, 'and it all worked out just the same.'

'Yes, living with their parents instead of in a home of their own. And that can be a recipe for disaster, with the mother ruling the roost and using the new bride like a servant in the house.'

'There's gloomy you are, Emo Rees! Your mam would never be like that, so don't go giving Dinah the wrong idea, boyo.'

Blushing, Dinah decided it was time to change the subject. 'I'm sure that Mum is very disappointed. When we were young we used to dress up in her own bridal veil that she'd kept wrapped up in tissue paper for all those years. She used to talk about the day when we would get married, wearing her veil, and the beautiful dresses she'd make for us. That didn't happen for Joyce.'

'Ah, but there's a war on, cariad,' Gwladys said, trying to smooth things over. 'Weddings aren't what they used to be, what with clothing coupons and food rationing and all. Your sister has saved your mam a lot of fuss and bother.'

'That may well be, but I know she'll never get over not being there to see Joyce walk down the aisle. Surely she could have waited just a few more days?'

Gwladys shook her head in puzzlement. 'Now then, our Emo, was there something you wanted? Did Bron send you with a message?'

'Just passing, Auntie.' They switched into Welsh while Dinah thought about what Emo had said earlier, about courtship in Bryncollen.

Young sweethearts went out walking together because there was little else to do here, apart from the occasional trip to the cinema. Well, she and Emo were doing that, on a rather informal basis, it was true, although she had gone with him to Swansea, for moral support,

Dinah had been to tea with Mrs Rees, and been kindly received. But she believed that had been under the guise of welcoming an evacuee teacher to the community. Could it have been more than that?

So far Emo had said nothing about wanting to meet Dinah's mother. Again, that could not be easily accomplished, with Mrs Blake so far away. And of course Dad was dead, so there was no father to demand to know if Emo's intentions were honourable.

With a sigh, Dinah wished she could be more like Tansy. That young woman would have no trouble finding out how a man felt about her. She might even declare her love for the man in question, thus giving him a cue to reciprocate. Dinah knew now that the one thing she wanted to hear was a declaration of love from Emlyn Rees!

'I think I'll go for a walk,' she said. 'I'm too jittery to settle to anything.'

'I should be going, too,' Emo remarked, 'so I'll walk along with you, if that's all right. It's getting dark and we don't want you walking into a lamp post and getting a black eye.'

As they strolled through the twilight she wondered if he would stop and kiss her again, but when they came to the fork in the road he only gave her a jaunty salute with his fingers half-way to his cap, and marched on.

★ ★ ★

At home in Coventry, Alice Blake went about her daily round as if in a fog. How had everything changed so quickly from the life she had known and enjoyed? Her days went past in a blur as she walked past one ruined house after another, on her way to the shops. Homes gone for good, and so many lives smashed with them. It was almost too much to take in. She longed to crawl into her bed, pull the covers over her head, and stay there, but one had to go on. To give in was to let that Hitler win.

Poor Joe. Her husband had been gone for many years, but she longed to have him by her side now. She supposed she could have remarried but that would have taken effort, and she had devoted all her time to bringing up

200

their two little girls; no easy task for a woman on her own. Now, though, she wished that she did have someone to turn to, someone to take charge and help her through the lonely days.

What would Joe have thought about the way things had turned out with Joyce? For the umpteenth time her thoughts turned to that day when the girl had come home, apparently risen from the dead. First there was joy, which soon turned to anger, and then puzzlement.

'How do I know you're really married?' she demanded.

Joyce held out her left hand again. 'See? Here's my ring.'

'That proves nothing. It could be a curtain ring from Woolworth's!'

'Harley said you wouldn't believe me. That's why I brought our marriage certificate for you to see.'

Alice took the paper without so much as a glance at it. 'Harley?' What kind of name is that? Where I come from men are called George or Sid, or Joseph, like your father.'

'I think it's a nice name. Mrs Harley Parker, that's who I am now.'

'And where did you meet this Harley, pray?'

'He got on my bus one morning. I asked him where he wanted to go. 'Anywhere with you, love!' he said. 'I'd follow you to the ends of the earth.' Of course I told him we only went as far as the city centre, so he'd have to be content with that.'

'Well, that's a fine line of chat, I must say,' Alice grumbled angrily.

'Oh, most of the chaps on our route are like that, Mum! It's only a bit of fun, see. Passes the time of day.'

'But not all of them sweep you off your feet, I suppose.'

'Of course not. Harley was different. Anyway, he started coming on my bus every day and then he asked me out. It was so romantic, Mum.' Joyce's eyes were like stars. 'I've never met anyone like Harley before.'

'Evidently! And may I ask why you

didn't invite him home for tea, so I could meet him? That's the usual thing to do, you know.'

'Oh, Mum — you weren't here. You'd gone to Leamington.'

'Leamington is not the other side of the moon, my girl! You could have brought the man there, or sent me a postcard, asking me to come home.'

'There wasn't time. He was only in Coventry for a few days, on business, you see.'

'Funny sort of business if he had time to sit on a bus all day. If he's a businessman, what was he doing on a bus — doesn't he have a car?'

'You know that petrol is rationed, Mum. Haven't you see the posters? *Is Your Journey Really Necessary?*'

They were going round in circles. Alice looked at the certificate now, taking in the fact that the couple had been married in the local registrar's office. It seemed genuine enough, yet she felt that there was something fishy about the whole business. This Harley

Parker was forty-five years old to Joyce's twenty-one — almost Alice's age, if it came to that. If this didn't end in tears, Alice would eat her hat.

'Will you be going back to work on the buses?' she wondered.

'No, Mum. We're not staying in Coventry. Harley has been staying at a very nice country hotel, and he'll be taking me there.'

'A hotel! That'll be pricey.'

'It's not that sort of hotel. People he knows have a big house, and they've taken in a few select people who want to escape the bombing.'

'A boarding house. Your husband is taking you to live in a boarding house!' Alice rolled her eyes in frustration. 'That's no way to start a marriage. Look, why not bring him here? You can have Dinah's room. She's not likely to be back for the foreseeable future.'

Joyce ignored the suggestion. 'It's not a boarding house, Mum, not in the way you mean. It's a lovely old place, set in its own grounds. Harley says it was just a family home until war broke out, but then the people started taking in paying guests, in case the place was requisitioned by the government. Harley says that's happening all over the country now. Big houses are wanted as convalescent homes for wounded men, or for government offices that are being evacuated from London. I thought you'd be glad to know I'm tucked away safely in the country.'

'Uh huh,' was the only reply she got.

'Well . . . so . . . that's it then, Mum. I have to dash. Harley's meeting me at the station, and off we go.'

Alice managed to pull herself together as she drew her foolish little daughter into a tight embrace. There was so much more she wanted to say, but in these uncertain times it didn't do to 'part brass rags' as they said in the Navy. People going on a journey never knew if they were seeing their loved ones for the last time.

★ ★ ★

So that's how we left it, Alice wrote to Dinah. *It's bad enough our Joyce getting married to a man she barely knows. That certainly wasn't wise, but what I can't understand is why she didn't bring the chap to meet me. There's something not right about this. The worst of it is that I completely forgot to ask for the address of the place where she's gone to live, so I can't even get in touch if I have to. I tell you this, Dinah Blake, if you ever do something like this to me, I'll never forgive you.*

Having read her mother's letter for the third time, she shared the contents with Gwladys, who had been waiting with bated breath.

'I can see why your poor Mam is worried, cariad,' she sympathised. 'But what's done is done. What God hath joined together, let no man put asunder.'

'It wasn't God joined them, it was a man in the registrar's office.'

'One way or the other, they're wed in the eyes of the Lord, Dinah.'

'But why the rush? Oh, I do hope she's not . . .'

'In trouble? Na, na, too early to tell, if she was. It's this war, see. Everybody rushing to get married while there's still time, in case something happens to one of them. Of course, you know the old saying: marry in haste, repent at leisure. What happens if both parties come through the war only to find they've nothing left to say to each other, see? Stuck with each other they'll be then, until death do them part.'

'But why did she do it, Mrs Richards? Going off with a man twice her age. I mean, Joyce has always been a bit flighty, but she had plenty of chaps her own age to choose from. Why couldn't she pick one of them?'

'Perhaps that's the attraction, cariad. She never knew your da, did she, poor girl? Now she likes the feeling of having someone to protect her, see,' Gwladys offered.

'Well, I certainly wouldn't marry a man as much older than me as that,' Dinah said with a shudder.

Gwladys gave her a sly look. 'And you won't have to, cariad! Just three years older than you, is our Emo, see!'

Dinah blushed. She couldn't bring herself to respond to this. If she said that she had no notion of marrying Emlyn Rees it would be a lie. She realised now that she would like nothing better than to spend the rest of her life with her handsome Welshman. She was irrevocably in love with him now — head over heels in love!

If only he felt the same way about her! If she could get him to propose to her in time for the Easter holidays she could take him to Coventry to meet Mum. The two of them would get on so well. They would not be able to get married at once, of course. In fact they might even have to wait until the war was over and the country was getting back to normal.

She wouldn't care about that. It would be enough to know that her future lay with Emlyn Rees.

Daydreaming, Dinah wondered where the wedding would take place. Usually this happened in the bride's local church, of course. She'd love to be married in Coventry, a place she loved, but who knew if the church she'd attended as a child would still be standing if there were any more air raids? And all her old school friends had long since scattered, some to join the forces, others to train as nurses or teachers. She had lost touch with them all. Her two colleagues here were her friends now.

Bryncollen, then. Would Emo agree to having the ceremony in the Anglican church, to which their little school was attached? She could just see herself coming down the aisle as his new wife.

Gwladys Richards appeared at the door, dustpan and brush in hand, to break into Dinah's reverie. 'I was wondering, was you going to be in here all day, cariad . . . ? Only I want to get started on this room, see.'

The magnificent daydream shattered, Dinah smiled resignedly, gathered up her books and left the room.

12

Dora spent a sleepless night, with her thoughts going round and round. It wasn't so much the idea of fighting her way through this mess with Paisley Oattes that she found upsetting; all she needed to do was to refuse outright to give the girl the money she wanted. Things might become unpleasant, but she could always go to the police if the worst came to the worst, and if she kept her wits about her, that probably would not be necessary.

She had a shrewd suspicion that this was some kind of scam. As Sian kept saying, some people took advantage of tragedies to feather their own nests. Dora herself remembered the time when a neighbour had died and someone had broken into the house while everyone was away at the funeral. The police had never managed to trace the culprit and the woman's daughters lost all the little knick-knacks, family heirlooms, which their mother had wanted them to inherit.

What really distressed Dora was the idea that her husband had fathered a child without her knowledge. If the girl was telling the truth, she was going to be nineteen in a few month's time. That meant she was born in . . . what . . . 1922? Where would Jim Ramsey have been then? He and Dora had been married in 1924, when he was twenty-three, and Dora a year younger. He could have known this girl Paisley's mother — and had an intimate relationship with her.

Had he known about the child? Surely he would have confessed such an important part of his past to Dora before their wedding? Had he kept in touch with the woman after he was married? If any of this was true, then Jim Ramsey wasn't the man whom Dora thought she knew.

And how was she to find out? It

wasn't the sort of thing you could ask in a letter. She could imagine him reading such an epistle. The anger darkening his face as he realised that his wife didn't trust him enough to dismiss this accusation out of hand.

That, of course, was if he was innocent of all charges — but what if they were true? He would still be upset at being found out after all these years. Either way it could be dangerous. Soldiers trained with guns, didn't they? What if he had an accident?

No, it certainly wasn't wise to interrogate him on paper, anything of the sort would have to wait until he came on leave, and goodness knew when that might be. She could, of course, wait until the Easter holidays and go in search of him, but that was some way off.

Meanwhile, she had questions to ask Paisley Oattes.

★　★　★

True to her word, the girl returned the following day. Dora had no idea where Paisley had spent the night and she didn't much care.

The girl curled her lip when Dora began to talk. 'You don't have to go on at me like I'm one of the kids in your class. I have my rights, and our mam told me I'm to make sure I get what's due to me.'

'My dear child, of course I want answers. You turn up here out of the blue trying to get money out of me, and you can't expect me to hand it over without a qualm. As far as I can see, you have absolutely no proof that my husband is your father.'

'I showed you the snap, didn't I?'

'And that proves nothing. Perhaps he and your mother did know each other, many years ago, but that's a far cry from saying that they had a child together. What is her name, by the way?'

'Rose. Rose Oattes. And if you're insinuating that my mother is a loose woman . . . '

'Of course I'm not. But she obviously had a relationship with somebody, and if it wasn't my Jim then it had to be someone else.'

'It was James Ramsey, I tell you! Mam said so!'

'When did she tell you this? When you were little? Perhaps you simply misunderstood.'

'I told you yesterday. I thought Gran was my mam. Mam only told me the truth after Gran died. Actually it was a neighbour who spilled the beans. Met me in the street and said she was sorry my gran died. It seems she'd known all along, that neighbour did, or guessed. It came as a shock to me, I can tell you. I went home and had it out with Mam.'

Dora's heart went out to the girl. 'And that's when she mentioned Jim's name?'

'Not at first. She hummed and hawed a bit, and then she came out with it. We never talked about it again until the big air raid came, and we lost everything. Then she started talking about him again, like she couldn't stop. Said they'd been so much in love, but she was only eighteen at the time and didn't have a clue about anything. She was a barmaid at the Dog and Duck back then, and Jim used to come in with his mates, and have a laugh and that. When he asked her out she was over the moon, and it all went on from there.'

'And that was when she said you should find your father?'

'Yes. 'He'll have to look after us now,' that's what she said.'

'Didn't you think it strange that she should turn to him now, after all these years? It's not as if he's been involved in your lives recently, is it?'

The girl shrugged. 'That's Mam's business. She doesn't like me asking a whole lot of questions.'

I bet she doesn't, Dora thought. 'Do you have your birth certificate with you, by any chance? I'd like to see it.' She waited while the girl fiddled with her shabby handbag. She didn't really think that Jim's name would be on the certificate; usually in these cases the registrar put down 'father unknown'. Still, what was actually written there came as a shock to Dora.

Father, Percy Oattes, porter. Mother, Annie Oattes, nee Marlowe. Child, Paisley Anne Oattes, born at Coventry May 27th, 1922.

'Who are these people — your grandparents?'

'That's right.'

So the couple had made a false return, which was an offence under the law. Not that it mattered now, when, according to this girl, they were both deceased. They had obviously done this to protect their daughter and grandchild, but in effect they had saved Paisley's father, whoever he was, from any legal retribution. Not that it absolved the man from any moral obligation.

'I'm sorry,' she said firmly, 'but nothing you've been able to tell me has convinced me that my husband should give you money. In any case, he isn't here now to do anything about it, even if he feels he should.'

'You're his wife. You can give me something on account.'

'I'm sorry, I don't have anything to spare. I had a bit saved up but I sent it to the Red Cross when Coventry was blitzed.'

'You must have been paid since then.'

'That's my business,' Dora returned firmly. 'You'll have to wait until the Easter holidays. If I can get away I'll try to see my husband, and possibly your mother as well. Until then, I'm afraid my hands are tied.'

'You haven't heard the last of this, don't think you have!' the girl shouted. 'You can be made to hand it over, you'll see!'

'That's called demanding money with menaces, my girl. I'll pretend I didn't hear that. I'll have to ask you to leave now. I must get to school.'

Her face red with fury, Paisley flounced out of the house. Dora put her hands to her chest, as if trying to slow her throbbing heart.

'Well, I hope you didn't part with any cash,' Sian said, coming into the room with a duster in her hand. 'I know her sort. Always on the cadge.'

'I can't help feeling sorry for her,' Dora said. 'She's been through a lot, finding out that nothing in her background is as she always believed it to be and now she's lost her home, her job and all her possessions.'

'So have a lot of other people, and don't you forget it. That Hitler flattened your home too, not to mention you've had to leave everything behind and come here to Bryncollen with all those children.'

'That's true,' Dora conceded.

'And what if this girl is telling the truth, as she knows it? It could be the mother who is spinning a web of lies. It seems funny to me that she's never bothered with the father of her child all these years until she wants to get something out of him. I don't like the smell

219

of this, Mrs Ramsey, and that's a fact.'

'I've thought of all that, and I don't intend to part with any money, especially on so little evidence. But it's my Jim I'm thinking of. We've been married for seventeen years and we always seemed to rub along all right. We've had our ups and downs, what couple doesn't? But I always believed there were no secrets between us. Now it looks as if our marriage has been a sham all along, and I can't bear it!'

'Now, now, enough of that!' Sian said soothingly. 'He's your hubby, and you have to have faith in him.'

'But what if he's been carrying on with this Rose Oattes behind my back all along?'

'Is that likely? With all of you living in the same town? Someone would have noticed and told you about it before now.'

'But Coventry is a big place . . . ' Dora did not want to believe that Jim Ramsey had played her false, but she could not get the thought out of her mind.

13

Brian Williams groaned as he saw his wife advancing on him. What now? Sybil was always coming up with some 'little job' she wanted him to do. 'I want to talk to you, Brian,' she announced.

'Can't it wait? I was just going down to the newsagent's. That wretched boy failed to bring my *Times* yet again.'

'This is important, Brian. Come and sit down.'

With a sigh he followed her into the drawing room. 'Well, what is it?'

'I want you to go to Brynamman and see Ceinwen Pugh.'

'What for? I told you I paid her off, and quite handsomely, too. I thought that would be the end of it. Don't tell me that Philip is seeing the girl again. I won't have it, Sybil!'

'As far as I know he hasn't seen her since.'

'Then what is this all about?'

'I want to bring baby Owain here to live. He is our grandson, after all.'

'If indeed he *is* Philip's son. I've always had my doubts about that.'

'I'm well aware that the boy can do no wrong in your eyes. He's always been your favourite. But the girl swore that he's the father, and I believe her,' Sybil said firmly.

'Why now? You wanted nothing to do with the child in the beginning.'

'It's just that I've been thinking . . . there's a war on, Brian.'

'I have noticed.'

'There's no need to be sarcastic. Our sons are in the forces now and every one of them could be killed, or badly wounded. In that case there would be no new generation to carry on the estate.'

'Now you listen to me. If the worst happens and our sons don't come home again, do you think this place will matter two hoots to me after that? Leave things as they are, and forget about bringing a little cuckoo into the nest.'

His wife stood up and began to pace about the room, agitated. 'I'll remind you that this place means the world to me, too. It's been in my family for two hundred years, and if there's any cuckoo in the nest it's you, Brian Williams!'

'I say, old girl!'

'Yes, well, I'm sorry. I shouldn't have said that, but you only came into the place when you married me. It stands to reason you don't feel the same as I do. Of course I hope and pray with every fibre of my being that the boys will come home safely, but we must face facts. That's why I want little Owain to be brought up here, you see.'

'I had the impression that the girl is very fond of the little chap. I very much doubt she'd give him up so easily,' he told her. 'And before you suggest paying her off again, the answer is no. I'll have no part of buying a child from its mother.'

'Don't be so melodramatic. Of course the girl will come here, too. You don't suppose I'd start bringing up a small child at my age, do you? And why go to all the expense of hiring a nanny when he has a mother?'

'I don't know about this. I'll need time to think.'

'Well, don't leave it too long. I've heard that the billeting officer is going round again, trying to place more evacuees, from Swansea, this time. We managed to avoid that last time because the house was full up, but now, with the boys gone, we have three spare bedrooms. Which would you rather have — your own grandson staying with us, or some city urchins racing around the house, breaking all my ornaments?'

'She won't want to come, you know, leaving her family to live under the same roof as a disapproving mother-in-law.'

'I'm hardly her mother-in-law, nor ever will be, if I have any say in the matter. As for disapproval, I hear that her father is a stalwart of the chapel. I don't suppose he thinks much of his girl giving birth out of wedlock. You get the car out and go to Brynamman this morning.'

'We're not supposed to waste petrol.'

'Phooey. You're a magistrate, aren't you? If you can't drive a few miles for something as important as this, I don't know who can. Go get your jacket and get going. You can collect your newspaper on the way.'

Muttering to himself, Brian Williams did as he was told. Anything for a quiet life. He hoped that nobody would be at home in the miner's cottage when he arrived, and then he could turn the car round and return to Bryncollen. By that time Sybil might have thought better of her crazy plan.

Unfortunately for him, the Pugh home was filled to overflowing with people when he reached there.

'What do you want?' Ellis Pugh demanded, when he saw who his visitor was. 'We said all we had to say the last time you was here, see.'

'May I speak to you in private? I have a proposition to put to you.'

'Proposition, is it? Fine words, Mr Williams. We have no secrets here, unlike some. Speak in front of us all, or not at all.'

'Won't you sit down, sir?' Pugh's timid wife indicated a chair which she hastily dusted off with a flick of her apron. Williams sat down, joined by Ellis Pugh and his two strapping sons. Mrs Pugh remained standing, hovering anxiously in the background.

Of the baby there was no sign; sleeping in another room, probably, or taken out in its pram by the girl, who did not seem to be here either. No, not a pram, he corrected himself. Those were for better-off people, such as himself. Miners' wives and daughters carried their infants inside big shawls which they wore over their own shoulders, enveloping both mother and child.

'I really came to speak to Ceinwen,' he began.

'She's not here,' Pugh snapped. 'Gone to visit her married sister, see. You can tell me what you come for, and — only if it's worth repeating, mind — I'll pass it on.'

Williams took a deep breath. 'I've come to offer your daughter and the baby a home, Mr Pugh.'

'She's already got a home, mister.'

'Please, Ellis, just wait and see what he has to say,' Mrs Pugh pleaded, resting a hand on her husband's shoulder.

'Owain is our grandson, Mr Pugh. My wife would very much like to have him living with us, now that our sons have joined up. Naturally we couldn't think of separating mother and child, so Miss Pugh would be made welcome as well.'

'Welcome, is it? That wasn't the way you put it before, when you come here with your blood money.'

'We were all in shock at the time. No father likes to think that his son is capable of behaving badly and Philip is our youngest child. His mother has always been particularly protective of him. And what I gave you wasn't blood money, as you put it. We genuinely wanted to contribute to the baby's expenses.'

'And glad to get it, we were, when Ceinwen couldn't work, and no money coming in,' Mrs Pugh said, nodding. Her husband flapped a hand in her direction.

'That's enough out of you, woman! I'll do the talking here.'

'Now that we've had time to think things over,' Brian went on, 'we believe that we should have acted differently. And surely Miss Pugh should decide for herself whether this is what she wants for the boy?'

'I shall decide,' Ellis Pugh declared. 'Ceinwen will do as she's told, see. Come you back a week from today, and you shall have my answer.'

Defeated for the moment, Brian Williams left the house and returned to Bryncollen. His wife was watching from the hall window as he drove up. She bounced out onto the drive, her eyes wide.

'Well? What transpired? Are they coming?'

'I don't know yet. She wasn't at home when I called, and the father was none too helpful. I'm to go back next week and I'll find out then if the girl wants to come.'

'Of course she'll want to come! Crammed into that poky house with all those people, she'll be glad to get into a place where there's a separate nursery for little Owain.'

'This house may seem like a palace to her at first, Sybil, but there's nothing to say that she'll want to stay here. If she decides she wants to go back to her own family, there's nothing we can do to stop her.'

'Then you must make her sign something to say the baby stays with us, Brian. See your solicitor and get him to draw up the papers.'

'I'm not sure that would be legal, my dear.' Brian sighed.

'That's why you have a solicitor, isn't it? To advise you of our rights.'

'And the mother's rights,' he murmured, but his wife wasn't listening. She had already gone to the nursery to see what was needed to prepare for Owain's coming.

★ ★ ★

Peter Williams seemed quieter than usual, and Tansy wondered why. Not that she minded much; it was pleasant strolling through the woods, listening to the birds calling. The dog raced from one place to another, stopping to sniff at every new scent and now and then lifting his leg to define his territory.

'Is there anything wrong?' she asked, when ten minutes had elapsed without a murmur. 'You seem to have something on your mind.'

'What? Oh, sorry! I'm not being very good company, am I?'

'I just wondered if you were worried. You seemed so far away.'

'Not worried, exactly. Only a bit concerned. I've had my orders. I'm to report to St Athan's on Monday, to start pilot training on Hurricanes.'

'But that's what you wanted, isn't it?'

'Of course. I'm pleased about that. I can't wait to get started, and then it's Hitler, watch out!'

'What is it, then?'

He hesitated for a moment and then asked, 'Have you heard from Philip lately?'

Tansy frowned. 'No. Why? I didn't think you minded my writing to your brother. I promised him I'd keep in touch, but I expect I'm only one among a horde of female friends, really.'

'It's not that. I wondered if he'd said anything, that's all.'

'For goodness' sake, Peter! You're talking in riddles! Spit it out, why don't you?'

He laughed. 'All right then. Here it comes. Some time ago Philip got a girl into trouble, that is, she had a baby. He refused to take responsibility, but Dad

231

made a payment to the girl's family on Phil's behalf.'

Tansy already knew this via the Bryncollen grapevine. 'And you think I should be warned, in case he tries anything with me?'

'Good grief, no! I'm sure you're old enough to look after yourself.'

'Thanks a lot, Peter!' Tansy shot him a look.

'I'm sorry, that didn't come out right. What I'm trying to say is that Mother has got it into her head that we're all going to be killed in action, or die of wounds or something. So if that happens she wants to make sure that the line is carried on. In other words, she wants Owain — that's his name — to inherit. She's inviting the boy and his mother to live with her and Dad. It's more in the line of an order, I think, knowing Mother.'

'That's good, isn't it? If that's what the girl wants, I mean.' Personally Tansy felt that the girl would be mad to move in with Sybil Williams. A snootier woman she had yet to meet.

'Oh, I don't know. It's as if we three have been written off already, you know. I understood that going off to war is no piece of cake, but this has made me take a long hard look at my own mortality.'

'I see . . . ' Tansy began to understand.

'So I've decided to get married. I'll have somebody to come home to on leave, and with any luck I'll eventually have children to come after me when I'm gone.'

Tansy's heart suddenly plummeted. 'Who is the lucky lady?' she asked, through stiff lips.

He looked at her as if she'd gone mad. 'Why, you, of course! Who did you think I was talking about?'

'Me?' she squeaked. 'Is this a proposal, then? It's not what I'd call romantic, Peter!'

'I'm sorry, Tansy. I'm not one for all this hearts and flowers stuff, but if it means that much to you we'll go out to a restaurant tonight and I'll say it properly then. In the meantime, will you marry me, Tansy Smith?'

'I couldn't marry someone who doesn't love me, Peter . . . '

'But of course I love you, Tansy. I wouldn't ask you otherwise!'

'You could have fooled me. From your remarks just now I thought you wanted me to be the little woman waiting at home for hubby to return. The pregnant woman, moreover. That's a pretty tall order, considering the fact that you haven't even kissed me yet.'

Nothing if not willing, he moved closer, about to take her into his arms, but she dodged away.

'So you're turning me down, then, are you?' he demanded, his expression reminding Tansy of a puppy who has just been scolded for chewing the carpet.

'I didn't say that. Look, I need time to think this through. I can't say yes or no until I've worked it all out in my head.'

'But we don't have long, Tansy,' he

pleaded. 'I have to report to the RAF camp on Monday.'

'Can you meet me here directly after school tomorrow? One way or the other, I'll have an answer for you then.'

★ ★ ★

To say that Tansy's thoughts were in a whirl would be an understatement. It seemed an age since she had met the three Williams brothers and seen their lovely house. Back then, she had been determined to win one of them for a husband, and she hadn't cared much which one. Now, faced with victory, she thought she must have been out of her mind to contemplate entering what would amount to a marriage of convenience, simply to win a better life for herself.

She had just reprimanded Peter for not loving her, or at least being unable to express such feelings. *Hypocrite* she told herself. *You don't deserve a good husband, Tansy Smith.* Nevertheless, she could marry Peter Williams if she chose to do so, and surely all the marriages in the world were not based on a grand passion? There must be many where the couple led a quiet existence, supporting each other in their daily lives.

She sat down on the trunk of a fallen tree, despite the angry chattering of a squirrel nearby. 'It's all very well for you,' she told it. 'The only decision you ever have to make is where to hide your acorns, or whatever it is you like to eat.'

She looked over her shoulder, to make sure that she was alone. It wouldn't do for any of her pupils to overhear her talking to herself, like a crazy woman. But she couldn't bring herself to go back to her lodgings just yet. Her landlady would probably make some snide remark about Tansy getting above herself by walking out with one of the wealthy Williams brothers. The woman had said it all before.

If only there was someone to confide in! As an older, married woman, Dora

Ramsey seemed like the obvious choice, but she had seemed strangely distracted recently. Her husband was in the Army; perhaps they were sending him abroad, and Dora was worried about his safety.

As for Dinah Blake, she was a shy little thing who probably hadn't even been kissed in her life. There was no use talking to her about love. Her head was probably full of romantic notions gleaned from reading novels, where at the end of the story the hero and heroine walked hand in hand into the sunset together. Those books never told you how difficult life could be when the wedding was long past, and you were trying to make sixpence do the work of a shilling, as Tansy's mother had to do.

And that sort of poverty-stricken existence was precisely what Tansy had vowed to avoid, and why she was in such a dilemma now.

Peter Williams was the strong, silent type, and a man she liked very much. They were good friends now, and she could do worse than marry him. She had long ago given up on his elder brother, Paul, who had inherited his mother's unpleasant snobbery. As for Philip, she had soon seen through him!

She attempted to project her thoughts into the future. Say she agreed to marry Peter. He was leaving within days, so there wasn't time for that to happen before he went. They would have to wait until he was given leave, and then there would be one of those war-time weddings with the groom in uniform and the bride wearing borrowed finery. And afterwards?

She certainly wouldn't stay on with Mrs Matthews! Apart from anything else it wasn't the sort of place where you could bring a husband, coming home on leave. Would Peter expect her to move in with his parents? Living with Sybil Williams would be jumping out of the frying pan into the fire, with a vengeance!

Suddenly, she knew what she had to do.

When she met Peter the following afternoon he was obviously on tenterhooks,

238

wondering what she meant to say to him.

'Well? Have you decided? Are you going to marry me, Tansy?'

'Yes, Peter, if you still want me.'

'Darling!' He pulled her into his arms and gave her a warm, lingering kiss. 'You'll never be sorry, I promise you. Now then, what shall we do about the wedding? I wonder if there's time to get a special licence, so that we can marry before I go?'

Tansy drew herself slightly away from him. 'I've been thinking about that, Peter. We haven't known each other all that long. I think we should just get engaged for now. After all, there is a war on. Nobody knows what the future may hold.'

'I thought you might say that, Tansy, so I've come prepared.' Putting his hand in his jacket pocket he pulled out a small, velvet-covered box. Snapping it open, he revealed a beautiful diamond ring, sparkling in the late afternoon sunlight.

14

In April Coventry was bombed again, for two nights in a row. The three teachers, who had gone to the cinema together to see a re-run of *Gone With the Wind,* starring Vivien Leigh and Clark Gable, watched the newsreel with tears in their eyes.

'Poor old Coventry,' Dora mourned.

'I could kill that Hitler!' Tansy shouted, and for once nobody turned around to say shush.

'I wish somebody would!' countered a small, fierce-looking woman, and for once they were all in agreement.

Dora, who had already seen the film twice before, let her mind wander. She had already come to terms with the loss of the little house where she and Jim had spent most of their married life, but Tansy and Dinah had more to worry about. Tansy's family were still in

Coventry, homeless; pray Heaven none of them had been hurt or killed this time. Dinah's mother was still there, as far as anyone knew. Nobody on her street possessed a telephone, so it would be some time before news eventually reached Bryncollen.

Two days later Dinah received a letter, the address in Alice Blake's familiar handwriting.

'Thank goodness, Mum's all right,' she told Emo, as she skimmed over the first page. 'She says here that the raids were pretty nasty, with hundreds of planes coming over, but somehow she escaped, even though she had to spend the night under the kitchen table.'

'There's glad you must be, cariad. Does she say anything else, like?'

Dinah turned over the page, and gasped.

'What is it? Is your home gone?'

'It's Mr Pepper, our headmaster. He's dead.'

'There's bad. Does Mrs Ramsey know?'

'I don't think so. Mum says here that his niece called round. She didn't know the address here, and she knew that Mum would.'

'Killed by a bomb, was he?'

'No, apparently not. He was in the Home Guard, you know, and it seems he had a heart attack while he was helping to dig a poor woman out of the rubble. He died before they could even get him to hospital.'

'Did you know him well?'

'As well as any beginning teacher knows her headmaster, I suppose. He was always kind and helpful to me. I can't believe he's gone. Now I'll have to go and break the news to Mrs Ramsey. I'd better do it now, before I lose my nerve.'

'I'll come with you, cariad, to give you a bit of moral support.'

Dinah felt a warm glow. It was so good to have someone to lean on at a time like this.

They found Dora helping her land-lady to wind knitting wool. The skein was looped over her two hands, while the other woman quickly wound the yarn into a ball. Sian greeted Emo with amusement.

'Hello, Emo! Come to lend us a hand, is it, boyo?'

'Na, na, Mrs Llewellyn. That's women's work, that is. I'm better at handling wool while it's still on the sheep,' he said gravely. 'We're the bearers of bad news, I'm afraid.'

'There's terrible, bach! It's not your mam, I hope?'

'Or yours, Dinah?' Dora gulped, having seen Dinah's white face.

Dinah swallowed a sob. 'It's Mr Pepper,' she blurted. 'He's dead.'

'Oh, tell me that's not true! It was in that beastly air raid, I suppose.'

Dinah nodded. 'I've had a letter from Mum. Mr Pepper's niece went round to see her because she didn't have our addresses here.' She went on to explain what the letter had said.

'The poor old boy,' Dora murmured. 'At least he had a good innings, I suppose. He was past retirement age, you know, but like me he came back to Soper Street when the war broke out.'

'At least he died a hero, Mrs Ramsey. Perhaps they'll give him a medal, post . . . post . . . whatever it's called.'

'Posthumously, Miss Blake, And no, I doubt there will be any medals for Mr Pepper. His story is not unique, I'm sorry to say. But he'd be pleased to know that he'd saved the life of someone else; I'm sure of that. Did the woman survive, the one he was trying to help?'

'Mum didn't say. Oh, well, we can't stop, Mrs Ramsey. I just felt I should pass on the news as soon as possible.'

'Thank you, Miss Blake. Will you be going to let Miss Smith know?'

'I wouldn't know where to find her. Her fiancé is home on leave and she's spending every spare moment with him.'

'I had no idea that Miss Smith is engaged. Who is it — someone she knows in Coventry?'

'Why, no. I assumed she'd told you long ago. It's Peter Williams.'

Sian dropped the ball of wool she was holding. 'Not Sybil Williams' son? I don't believe it! I think she's spinning you a tale, love.'

'No, honestly, it's true. I've seen her ring, a lovely diamond solitaire. She wears it on a chain round her neck.'

'If that means what I think it means, then his mam don't know about it yet,' Sian said.

'I don't think it's been announced in the paper, if that's what you mean,' Dinah replied.

'Obviously not, if his mam's still going around with her hair on!'

'Why should Sybil Williams object to her son marrying?' Dora said, speaking more in support of her young colleague than anything. Privately she knew quite well why the snobbish Sybil might object to Tansy. She was a wealthy woman, the wife of a magistrate, and the queen bee of Bryncollen. Her home and the estate had been in her family for centuries; no doubt she felt she had a position to keep up.

Tansy Smith, on the other hand, came from the back streets of Coventry, her decent, hard-working family as poor as church mice. That should not make any difference, for Tansy had worked hard to fit herself for a worthwhile profession. Unfortunately it did, for people in society practised one-upmanship, and woe betide any outsider who tried to rise into their ranks.

'Peter Williams? I thought it was the youngest one, Philip, she had her eye on. They seemed very chummy when Mrs Williams gave that welcome party for us last year.'

Sian began winding her wool again. 'She's had a narrow escape there. Young Mr Philip is one for the ladies, see. It was him got that poor girl in trouble, and I know that for a fact.'

'What girl?'

'Oh, Mrs Ramsey, you are behind the times and no mistake. Ceinwen Pugh is her name. She's living up at the

Williams place now, with Owain, her little boy, see.'

'Are you saying that Philip Williams is the father?' Dora gasped.

'Why else would Brian Williams let them over the doorstep? And I tell you something else, Mrs Ramsey . . . '

It was obvious that the two women were about to settle into a good gossip, so Dinah politely excused herself and left them to it, with Emlyn close behind her.

'And there's something else that nobody knows, Mrs Ramsey. Sybil Williams is putting pressure on Mr Williams to see about adopting the child formally, see. He's hemming and hawing about it but she'll win in the end. She always does.'

'But you said that nobody knows.'

'Ah, well. My cousin's girl works in the house, you know, and she hears things, see.'

'Then I hope they don't catch her eavesdropping on a sensitive conversation, or she'll be out on her ear.'

'Na, na. She'd never listen on purpose, Mrs Ramsey, but as she says, it's amazing what scraps of information you can pick up while you're flicking a duster about. People never notice servants, see. Next to invisible, they are.'

'But will the child's mother agree to that? Once she signs the papers that will be the end of it. She'll have no say in the boy's upbringing, and they could make it so uncomfortable that she'll want to leave. What will she do then? She won't have a leg to stand on.'

'That all depends. I've heard there's a chap courting her now, a man with a smallholding from up Glanamman way. A good marriage that would be, except that he wants no part of bringing up some other man's child, see.'

'Oh, dear! I hope she'll think twice about marrying him.'

'Aye, but look at it this way. If the Williamses take on young Owain, he'll always have the best of everything. He'll come in for a bit of a nest egg when his tadcu — his grandfather — dies, and what's wrong with that? On the other hand if she weds the farmer and they produce their own family, the boy will always be the odd one out, see. Maybe even treated badly by the stepfather. These things do happen, Mrs Ramsey.'

* * *

Tansy had taken to meeting Sybil Williams's housemaid in the wood during the light spring evenings. She hadn't wanted to at first, but the girl had come up to her and introduced herself when there was no escape.

'I'm Elin, Miss. Elinor, really, but everyone always just calls me Elin.'

'How do you do?'

'I know about you and Mr Peter, see?'

'So?' Tansy snapped. If this was the prelude to a blackmail attempt, she was having no part of it. She had asked Peter to keep their engagement a secret simply because she wasn't at all sure that she could go through with the marriage in the end. Therefore it was for the best that his mother should be kept in the dark. However, if the woman happened to find out, so be it.

'Oh, don't you worry, Miss. I can keep a secret. I'm on your side, see.'

'And what side would that be?'

'Well, it's you against the Williamses, isn't it? They're the high mucky mucks, and you're only ordinary, like me and Ceinwen Pugh. Not good enough for their precious son, are you?'

Tansy let that pass.

'I s'pose you haven't heard the latest, have you? It's Mr Paul. He's come home with a fiancée. Lady Mary, her name is. Titled, see.'

'That should please Sybil.'

'But poor little Ceinwen, she's wondering where this leaves her. Between the devil and the deep blue sea, she is. She wants to marry a chap who don't want her boy, but what if the Williamses don't want him any more, neither? Mr Paul's wedding is all set for September, see, and that means he

250

could have a son of his own by this time next year.'

'Or not, as the case may be,' Tansy muttered.

'I don't know what you mean, Miss.'

'Isn't it obvious? This Mary may be unable to have children, or they might only have daughters. Come to that, Paul could be killed in action before he gets time to father any child at all.'

'There's awful you are to say a thing like that!'

Tansy shrugged. 'There's a war on, you know, and like it or not, anything can happen.'

'My advice to you, Miss, is to marry Mr Peter the next time he comes home, to make sure you're in the running.'

Tansy sniffed. 'When I want your advice, I'll ask for it.'

'I know I'm speaking out of turn, Miss,' Elin said, not at all abashed, 'But once the mistress finds out what's going on she'll do everything she can to get rid of you, see. The master is one of the school governors and he can get you dismissed and run out of Bryncollen, just like that, see.'

Tansy doubted that, but she hesitated, and Elin kept on. 'So what I say is, don't even wait until Mr Peter comes on leave. You go to that place where he's stationed and get the chaplain to marry you. The old girl can't do nothing to you then, and neither can the old man. Think of the scandal if he tried to get rid of his own daughter-in-law.'

'I think that will be enough, Elin.' The naughty boys in her class had come to respect Tansy when she took that tone, and the maid heeded the reprimand, too.

'Then I'll say no more, Miss, but I'll keep my eyes and ears open and let you know what's going on up there. You'll thank me in the end.'

Tansy turned away. While recognising that Elin was a sly little thing and a born troublemaker, she realised that it might be just as well to keep abreast of developments in the Williams household. As for rushing off to St Athan to push Peter into marriage, she would do no such thing, even though he would probably welcome her with open arms.

It was good news about Paul, though. Sybil Williams would be so delighted at the prospect of having a titled daughter-in-law that she wouldn't mind so much when her second son declared his intention of marrying a girl who 'isn't one of us'.

And I'm not the slightest bit jealous of Lady Mary whatsit, Tansy told herself. *Even if Paul is the heir to the estate, I've never fancied him, not in the least.*

In fact, and much to her surprise, Tansy realised that she actually did love Peter. She lived for his letters, and sometimes when days went by without receiving one, she became anxious and despondent.

Perhaps she wasn't 'in love' in the way she had always imagined herself to be. Her heart didn't beat faster when she saw him coming. She didn't almost swoon with delight when he kissed her. This was something deeper and more lasting. Was it perhaps a case of absence making the heart grow fonder, now that he was miles away?

No, it was more than that. She had come to recognise in Peter Williams something that responded to a need in herself; he was kind and considerate and she believed that he would never let her down. Marriage to him might not be wildly exciting, but it would be safe and secure. And perhaps that was right and proper, once the excitement of the honeymoon had died down, and a couple settled in to everyday life. There would be children, of course, if they were lucky, and Tansy looked forward to that.

Teaching helped to pass the long days without him. She began to pay more attention to what went on in Bryncollen, for after all it would probably become her married home. At one time she had turned up her nose at the place, thinking of it as a temporary refuge until she could return to Coventry. The Welsh had been welcoming and it was a relief not to live in fear, but she had never lived in the country, and nor did she enjoy any country pursuits.

That Lady Mary was probably born on horseback, she though glumly. Tansy had had one ride on a seaside donkey at the age of three, and that was her only experience with horseflesh.

One day, exploring a lane that wound between tall hawthorn hedges, she came upon Dinah Blake and Emlyn Rees. They were strolling along, hand in hand, so engrossed in each other they failed to notice her at first.

'Well, well!' she said, as Dinah, blushing, withdrew her hand from Emo's grasp.

'What's all this, then? Sweethearts now, are we?'

'Not if you mean you and me, Miss Smith,' Emo retorted, with a gleam in his eye. 'Besides, a little bird tells me you're spoken for. We could plan a double wedding, eh? Although that might be difficult seeing as you're church and I'm chapel.'

'Dinah! Is this true? Are you two engaged? How wonderful!'

'Oh, don't listen to him; he's only joking,' Dinah spluttered, redder than ever with embarrassment.

'I don't know. I might get round to asking you yet,' Emo said, grinning. 'Not when there's strangers listening, though. I'd want to pick my moment, see?'

Tansy glared at him. 'If that's a joke, I don't think it's very funny! So long, Dinah. See you at school in the morning.' She stalked off, feeling annoyed on Dinah's behalf.

The girl was obviously smitten with the chap and very likely she had expectations. But what did he think he was doing, giving broad hints in public like that? If he wasn't sincere, it wasn't fair to get her hopes up.

Was that what she was doing with Peter? When he came home on his next leave, she would let him know that she did love him, and was looking forward to their wedding day. But what was it that the poet Robert Burns wrote? As far as she could remember, it was something about the best laid plans of mice and men not working out.

★ ★ ★

Walking to school the following morning she was surprised to see Elin running towards her, waving her arms like windmills. 'Miss Smith! Miss Smith! Wait! Stop!'

'What on earth is the matter?' Tansy demanded, when the girl stumbled to a halt in front of her. 'I really don't have time to chat now, Elin. I'm already late for school.'

'Oh, Miss! Oh Miss! You don't know, do you?'

'What don't I know?'

'The mistress had a telegram this morning. I think they said it's from the War Office, wherever that is. It's Mr Peter, Miss. He's been killed! Shot down in his fighter plane.'

Tansy grasped a nearby fence for support. 'I won't faint! I won't,' she muttered, as the world swam around her.

'Are you all right, Miss?'

'Of course I'm not all right, you fool! I've just heard that my future husband is dead! How do you expect me to feel?'

'Sorry, Miss, but I didn't want you to hear by accident, like. The news will be all round Bryncollen like wildfire, see?'

'Yes, I understand that, Elin, and I'm sorry I snapped.'

'I think you'd better go back to the house and take something to make you sleep. A good sleep is the best remedy for bad news, that's what our mam always says. Shall I go to the school and tell Mrs Ramsey what's happened?'

'No, no. I'll be all right in a minute. It's best to carry on as usual. Off you go, Elin, but if you hear anything more about what happened, will you come and tell me?'

'Yes Miss. I surely will. You can depend on me.'

15

When Dora arrived home after school on a gloomy Wednesday, she was greeted on the doorstep by her landlady, whose expression matched the weather.

'Is anything the matter, Mrs Llewellyn?'

'You've had a telegram. Better come in and sit down before you open it. Nasty things, telegrams.'

With a terrible feeling of disaster, Dora did as she was told. Everyone knew about the bad news recently received by the Williams family; only a few were aware that it affected Tansy Smith as well.

Sian hovered while Dora fingered the orange envelope. 'Is it about your hubby?'

Dora slit it open at last, and then she began to cry.

'What does it say? Is it bad news?

Don't move, Mrs Ramsey. Stay where you are and I'll fetch you a nice cup of tea.'

'It's Jim,' Dora said, brushing the tears from her face with the sleeve of her jacket. 'He's all right. He's coming on leave. He's got embarkation leave, he says.'

'Em . . . that means he's shipping out, doesn't it? Going to be in the thick of things in some nasty foreign place. The Army lets them come home to say goodbye, just in case . . . '

'Just in case they don't come back,' Dora finished for her. 'I wish there was some nice little place I could take him to, but there's not much hope of that. You can't find rooms for love nor money. Oh, well, I suppose it's all right for him to come here, Mrs Llewellyn?'

'I tell you what! I'll go and stay with my sister. It'll only be for a day or two, on account of the travelling taking up some of his time.'

'It's good of you to offer, but I can't think of driving you out of your own home,' Dora said.

'Na, na. It will be no trouble. Anyway, the pair of you need time to be alone together, see. You have things to discuss, remember.'

So it was all decided. Would she be brave enough to bring up the subject of the Oattes woman? It would be horrid to accuse him of anything during what could very well be their final days together. On the other hand, if the worst happened, that would leave her wondering for the rest of her life. Did he, or didn't he?

* * *

Jim, when he arrived, looked different; thinner in the face somehow.

'It's all the square-bashing they've got us doing,' he explained. 'It's knocked a few pounds off me, right enough. You haven't changed, love. Still the pretty girl I married.'

'I bet you say that to all the girls,' she said, laughing.

'Chance would be a fine thing. What

have you been up to while I've been away, then?'

As they sparred and joked, it was as though they'd never been apart. Dora made up her mind to avoid confrontation until the very last minute. But before long, their last evening arrived.

'Do you want to do something tonight?' Jim asked. 'There's a cinema here, isn't there? Do you want to go to the pictures?'

'Jim, we've got to talk.'

'Uh, oh! The words a husband always dreads to hear!'

'I'm serious, Jim. Something's come up, and we've got to get it straight between us before you go back.'

'They're not sending you back to Coventry, are they? I won't have it, old girl. It's far too dangerous there.'

'No, we're here for the duration, I think. This is about something else, although it does have to do with Coventry in a way.' She produced the snapshot from her handbag. 'Take a look at this.'

He peered at it. 'Well, I'll be blowed!'

'Do you recognise the people in it?'

'Of course I do.'

'Well, come on, then, out with it! Who is that girl on the left?'

'Well, it's a long time ago, love, but I believe that's Rose Oattes.'

Dora's stomach turned. 'And the other couple?'

'I vaguely recognise them, but I can't be sure. Just a couple of kids who lived down our street, I reckon.'

'And what were you doing on a beach with Rose Oattes?'

'Me? Don't be silly, love, that's Jack.'

'Jack? You mean your brother? I thought it was you.'

'People always said we looked like twins, but he was older then me. That's how he got into the last war while I was left at home. I've told you all this, haven't I? He was badly gassed when he was over there. He came back from France, but he was never the same afterwards. He hung on until 1921 before he eventually succumbed. It broke Mum's heart, you know, and she followed not long after.'

Jim stared at his wife as she began to put two and two together. 'But what's this all about, love? And where did that snap come from? I've never seen it before.'

Dora knew she had to tread carefully. 'A couple of months ago I had a visit from a nineteen-year-old girl who lives in Coventry. Paisley Oattes, her name is.'

'Oattes. Anything to do with Rose, then?'

'She's Rose's daughter, or so she says. And that's not all, Jim. She claims that you are her father. Her mother says that when she told you she was pregnant, you didn't want to know.'

Jim swore. 'I certainly hope you didn't believe that load of cobblers!'

'Of course not,' she lied, 'but it's raised so many unanswered questions. According to this girl she and her mother were bombed out, and they also lost their jobs as a result of the raids. They desperately need help, and so they were forced to turn to you.'

'Come off it, Dora! This is just a ploy to screw money out of us. I hope you haven't parted with your savings!'

'I'm not that stupid. It had worried me, though. Why did they pick on us, and how did they know where to find us?'

'It could be that our Jack really was the girl's father, or perhaps they just picked on him because he's not here to defend himself. Personally I think he was in no condition to get involved in a relationship with Rose, other than friendship. You should have seen the poor bloke, love; always heaving and gasping for breath. That's what gas does to you. I was sorry to see him die when he went, but he was well out of it, and that's a fact.'

'But Paisley's mum told her it was you.'

'Then she lied.'

'But why couldn't she just have said it was Jack?'

'How do I know? Let's face it, our

Jack isn't here to pay for his sins, but I'm still here.'

'Jim, do you swear to me that you had nothing to do with all this?'

'Of course, what do you take me for?' he answered incredulously.

'Then it doesn't make sense. You know you can't be the girl's father, so why would you hand over any money?'

'Ah, but I haven't been around, have I? It was you the girl came to, not me. They must have thought you'd be a soft touch.'

Dora thought for a while, digesting what Jim had told her. 'Of course, for all we know this was a scheme cooked up by the girl, and nothing to do with her mother at all.'

'You're forgetting her trump card — that snap. Rose must have hung on to that for years, the way you do with photos. The girl finds it in a drawer, picks it up and says 'Who are these people, Mum?' and Bob's your uncle.'

Dora still felt uneasy. 'The girl warned me she'd be back. I think she could get nasty and I don't want her causing a scandal here. Bryncollen is a very conservative place, Jim. For better or for worse I have to live here for the duration and I'd hate it if rumours got started. Look, I want you to go and see this Rose Oattes, and warn her off.'

'Sorry, love, no can do. If I don't report back on time I'll be in big trouble. Men who go absent without leave are dealt with severely especially in war time. You'll have to deal with it yourself.'

'But, Jim!'

'Wait until you're due a few days off, then go up to Coventry. Do it in the summer holidays if you have to. Track down where Rose Oattes is living, but don't rush in with all guns blazing. Ask around, first, talk to the neighbours. See what you can find out. If things look bad, you can always go to the police.'

'Are they likely to believe me?'

'You can but try. Otherwise you'll have to tackle the woman yourself. Now

267

let's forget all this nonsense, shall we? I'll be on my way in the morning and who knows when we'll be together again. Let's make the most of the time we've got left, shall we?'

He took her into his arms then, and she felt the cares of the world slipping away.

16

Despite the fact that there was a war on, Dinah felt young and carefree as the weeks went by. Mum was all right, despite the difficulties of daily life in bomb-ravaged Coventry. Everything was going well at school, where her charges had settled down happily into the slower pace of life in Bryncollen. And, best of all, her budding romance with Emlyn Rees was going swimmingly.

He was, she decided, a typical Celt with his black hair and eyes that sparkled when he was pleased with something. He wasn't a tall man, but that was just as well. Dinah was a mere five-foot-four in her bare feet and she wouldn't have felt comfortable walking about with someone who towered over her.

He had a marvellous tenor voice and he was in the habit of bursting into song at the most surprising moments. One day, when they were up on the hill overlooking the town, he suddenly broke into *You Are My Heart's Delight,* a piece made famous by Richard Tauber.

'Mum loves that song,' she told him. 'We always have to be quiet when that comes on the wireless.'

Emo smiled. '*And where you are, I long to be . . .* ' he continued.

Dinah smiled back. Had he chosen that song for a purpose? Was it directed towards her? She had learned that he wasn't good at putting his feelings into words, so was this his way of letting her know how he felt about her? If only she dared to ask him what it meant!

Perhaps it meant nothing at all. She had quickly learned that the Welsh were capable of singing at the drop of a hat, and not just in chapel, either. Even when they were queuing up at the shops, or to get into the cinema, someone always began singing, and before you knew it everyone else had joined in, with harmonies, descants, the lot!

His aunt was baking when Dinah arrived home.

'Is our Emo not coming in with you? There will be Welshcakes for your tea, although they won't be as good as they used to be, mind. I can't get the fruit, see. He likes a nice Welshcake, does our Emo.'

'He had something to do up on the estate. He says he may drop in later, if it's not too late when he's finished.'

'And how are things between you and Emo, cariad? Getting along nicely, are you?'

'I think so . . . '

'But you haven't named the day yet.'

'Well . . . he hasn't asked me to marry him . . . ' Dinah stammered.

'That's Emo all over. Backward in coming forward. Well then, you'll have to give him a nudge, see.'

'I couldn't possibly!' Dinah gasped, shocked.

'Then I'll have to do it for you.'

'Oh, please don't, Mrs Richards! It might put him off.'

'Na, na. I've seen the way he looks at you. Smitten, the boy is. And if that doesn't work you'll have to give him something to think about.'

'I don't know what you mean.'

'Plant the idea in his mind that he has a rival. Another man. That should bring him to the point in a hurry. Isn't there a young man back in Coventry, somebody you used to go out with? Just drop his name into the conversation once or twice, and see what happens.'

'I didn't have a boyfriend before I came here. I think I'm too quiet. Before I met Emo, men never seemed to notice me, or at least, not when my sister was around. She was the one everyone paid attention to because she's so bright and lively.'

'Not to worry; it's sure to come out in the wash, see.'

Comforted by her landlady's home-spun wisdom, Dinah went to her room, to prepare lessons for the coming week, but she found it hard to settle. Mentioning Joyce had made her think about her sister. She wondered how she was getting along. It was too bad that Mum didn't have her address, or she could write and ask her for a few tips on how to cope with Emo.

She had often noticed that you had only to think about some person or thing, to have them popping up out of the blue in the next little while. Thus she should not have been so surprised when Joyce arrived in Bryncollen on the following weekend.

'You have a visitor,' Gwladys Richards announced, when Dinah and Emo were barely through the door, after a long walk by the river. 'I put her in the front parlour with a cup of tea, me not knowing how long you two lovebirds were likely to be.'

'I'm not expecting anyone. It's not Tansy, is it?'

The door flew open and a distraught young woman immediately hurled herself into Dinah's arms.

'Joyce! What on earth are you doing here?'

'Don't scold me! I had to come!'

'Is your husband with you?'

'I never want to see him again!'

'Em . . . Mrs Richards, Emo . . . this is my younger sister, Joyce . . . '

'How do you do?' Emo said, looking at the sobbing girl who was now working up a head of steam, as his mother would have put it.

'I'd better be going, Dinah. I'll see you tomorrow,' he said.

'I'll see you out, boyo,' Gwladys said. 'I have a knitting pattern I promised to lend your mam. You can take it to her now, although where she'll come by enough wool, I don't know, mind. There's next to nothing in the shops.'

Left with Joyce, Dinah put on a stern expression. 'Now then, my girl, are you going to tell me what all this is about?'

'You sound just like Mum.'

'Do I? And I can just imagine what she's going to say when you land in there. It's such a cliché, Joyce, running home to Mother at the first sign of difficulty.'

'I can't go home,' Joyce wailed.

'It seems to me you don't have much choice. If you've left Charlie, where else can you go? There's a terrible shortage of accommodation all over the place.'

'Harley!'

'What?'

'Harley. That's his name, not Charlie. At least, that's what he told me. I found a letter in his overcoat pocket, addressed to Mr Harold Parker, and I'm sure that's what he's really called.'

'But surely you didn't leave him because of that?' Dinah was horrified. 'Lots of people change their names when they don't like the one they were christened with.'

'It wasn't just that. The whole thing was a great big sham from the beginning. I thought it was so romantic, Dinah, the way he kept turning up to see me, telling me he'd fallen for me like a ton of bricks. He said we were going to a lovely private hotel in the country, and after the war we'd get a place of our own with a garden and dogs. He was going to grow roses and he'd bring me a red one on my breakfast tray each morning, just to assure me of his love. That's what he said, Dinah, and it was lies!'

'I suppose we all have dreams, Joyce.'

'Dreams! Nightmares, you mean.'

'There wasn't a hotel after all? Where did he take you, then?'

'Oh, there was a hotel all right, but he wasn't a businessman, staying there as a guest. He was their porter cum gardener, just a servant.'

'That's good, honest work, Joyce . . .'

'Yes, and there was honest work for me, too. He'd signed me on as a housemaid, and I was expected to turn to and scrub floors and empty chamber pots! It was a terrible shock after all his promises, Dinah. The people were all right, and I didn't want to let on how I'd been deceived, so I went along with it for a while. Finally I couldn't stick it any longer, so I came away. I don't want him to find me, and he knows where Mum lives, so I came to you.'

'I suppose Mrs Richards will let you stay here for a day or two, if you've brought your ration book, but after that, like it or not, it's back to Coventry for you.'

'Mum will say 'I told you so'. I can't bear it, Dinah.'

'Don't worry about that now. Come upstairs with me, and I'll tuck you into my bed. You look as though you could do with a good rest.'

Dinah sat beside her sister until the girl dropped off to sleep. Poor, impulsive Joyce. She was too trusting, and that was how she'd landed in this mess. Married and separated, all in a matter of months.

Would Mum be sympathetic, or would she trot out old-fashioned maxims, telling her younger daughter that she had made her bed on the spur of the moment and must lie in it now?

Like her mother, Dinah, too believed that marriage was for life. If she married Emo, would they live happily ever after, or would they grow apart in time? He seemed truthful and sincere, but then so had Harley in the beginning, according to Joyce. Her poor sister had been badly taken in.

It was a classic case of not looking before you leapt, and Dinah would do well to learn from it.

* * *

Neither Tansy nor her family had ever been particularly religious, but now she spent long hours sitting in the church, even though it tended to be cold and damp. Somehow she derived comfort from being within its walls, and at first she wasn't sure why this was.

Then it occurred to her that the Norman structure must have seen much grief and joy over the centuries, and in that way she was not alone. Other women had sat where she was sitting, mourning the loss of men who had never returned from war.

There was nobody to share her thoughts with now. Dora seemed to have problems of her own, while Dinah was head over heels in love with her handsome Welshman, and good luck to her.

Tansy's mother and sisters might have been able to console her, but they were far away. In other circumstances it might have been possible to share Sybil Williams' distress, but the woman wasn't even aware that her son had been engaged to be married. If it was not for Elin, Tansy would have had no idea how Peter's parents were feeling.

'He wants to have a memorial service up the church,' Elin said. Tansy assumed that she was talking about Brian Williams.

'That's good, isn't it? I'll be able to take part in that. Presumably the whole of Bryncollen will be free to turn up.'

'Aye, but she won't have it, see. Or at least, not yet.'

'I wonder why?'

'Because she's still hoping he'll turn

279

up. I overheard them talking in the morning room when I was dusting. Well, I listened in on purpose, see, so I could tell you what's happening.'

Tansy could imagine the scene, as Elin gave her a blow by blow description . . .

★ ★ ★

'He could still come walking through that door,' Sybil muttered.

Her husband looked at her, his face sad. 'Now is that likely, when there were witnesses who saw his plane go down in the drink? We've got to face it, old girl. Peter is dead, and he won't be coming back.'

'He had a parachute, didn't he? He may have got out alive.'

'Don't you think we'd have heard by now, if he had?'

'He may have been taken prisoner, Brian. The Red Cross will be letting us know, any day now.'

Haunted by the reports of aircraft

280

going down in flames, spiralling out of control until the last, horrific moment, he gave his wife an uncharacteristic hug. She twisted out of his arms.

'This is all your fault, Brian Williams!'

'Steady on, old girl! How do you make that out?'

'You shouldn't have let him go into the Air Force. He'd have been better off in the Army. It's safer on the ground.'

He let that go without answering. As someone who had served in the trenches during the Great War he knew how untrue that was, but with two other sons in the Army now, it was best not to think about that.

'How could I have stopped him, Sybil? He's over twenty-one. Besides, if he hadn't volunteered he'd have been called up, and Heaven knows where they'd have placed him.'

'Flying lessons, Brian! You paid for those when he was so keen to learn to fly. Why I ever agreed to it, I can't think.'

Sadly, he left his wife to her grief.

She wasn't being reasonable, but then what wife or mother could be, after learning of an untimely death?

★ ★ ★

So Sybil Williams continued to lament her loss, while Tansy suffered in silence. One evening she was sitting in the church, staring unseeingly at the altar, when the sound of footsteps on the stone floor came to her ears. The vicar, perhaps, going about his daily round, or some member of the altar guild, come to do the flowers.

'Tansy Smith! Why are you sitting here, all alone in the dark? It's cold enough to freeze the tail off a donkey, even if it is almost summer!'

She swung around so quickly that she gave her arm a painful blow on the edge of the pew. She looked at the speaker and then, for the first time in her life, she fainted. When she came to she was lying in the pew, wondering for a moment where she was. She struggled to sit up.

'Peter! Oh, Peter! But they said you were dead!' A wave of dizziness washed over her. 'I think I'm going to . . . '

'I hoped you'd be glad to see me.'

Long moments passed while they embraced. Their kiss held so many varied emotions that Tansy could not decide whether it was passion, joy or relief she was feeling. When Peter was sitting beside her on the hard seat, with his arm around her shoulders, she at last found the breath to ask him what had happened.

'Did you manage to get out of your plane and parachute down to the ground, then? Was it in France, or over the Channel? Why couldn't you let anyone know right away that you were all right?'

'Whoa, steady on! I didn't contact anyone because it was a while before I knew I was dead.' Peter laughed. 'Sorry! That didn't come out right! What I meant was, I wasn't aware that I needed to let anyone know anything. The poor bloke who bought it was a Canadian, a Peter Williams from another squadron. We have a lot of Canadians over here now, belonging to the RCAF, and jolly good pilots they are, too. And of course I have a common enough name. There must be dozens of us in the services at the moment.'

'But I've heard that when someone gets killed in action, his commanding officer writes to the next of kin. He must have all the details, so why the confusion?'

'I daresay that the dead chap's CO did write to his people in Canada; my parents certainly didn't get any such letter. They received the usual War Office telegram and no doubt the Canadians are still waiting for official confirmation.'

'It's not right, Peter — someone should complain.'

'I'll write to Winston Churchill, then, shall I? Seriously, Tansy, with the way things are going at the moment it's no wonder there's chaos in some places.

Let's forget all that now, shall we?'

Tansy shuddered. *Until the next time,* she thought.

'Peter! Do you still want to marry me?'

He kissed her lightly on the top of her head. 'Of course I do. Did you think I might have changed my mind?'

'Then let's not wait any longer. Let's do it now. How long is your leave? Is there time to have the wedding before you go back?'

'I'll apply for a special licence. There's no time to have the banns read, but I take it you do want to have a church wedding, with all the trimmings? Perhaps a guard of honour outside, with all your little pupils holding up rulers or something?'

'There won't be time for all that. Couldn't we just elope?'

Peter's smile faded. 'There's nothing I'd like better, but it can't be done. It wouldn't be fair to my mother, you see, after she's just spent miserable days and nights thinking I was dead. Under the circumstances we can keep it small, but we must do the right thing, don't you see?'

Tansy nodded slowly. 'I don't suppose you've broken the news to your mother, have you? That you're engaged to me, I mean.'

'She'll be so overjoyed to find me alive, she'll welcome you with open arms, darling, don't you worry.'

Tansy doubted that, but she was ready to take on a dozen Sybil Williamses. Having discovered that she loved Peter, only to lose him, as she'd thought, she was taking no chances now.

'You'll want your mother here, won't you? I can help you out a bit if she can't afford the fare.'

'That's all right. I have some money saved up. Let's face it, there's not a lot to spend it on in Bryncollen. I'll dash off a letter to her tonight, and when I go to the post office tomorrow I'll get a postal order to put inside.'

'What about your father? Won't he

want to give you away?'

'I don't expect he'll be able to get off work. Anyway, he hates weddings. When my sisters were married Mum had the worst time just getting him into a collar and tie, and even then he grumbled all the way through the ceremony.'

'Do let him know he's welcome, though, won't you? I want us to start off on the right foot.'

Peter and Tansy were reluctant to part, but at last they went their separate ways. There was so much to talk about, so many plans to make for the future — but all that could wait.

Peter was alive, and Tansy was soon to wed the man she loved.

17

The school broke up for the summer holidays. Most of the pupils had made friends among the Welsh children and it was amusing to see the little boys drilling as if they were preparing for war. Broom handles and garden tools were used to simulate rifles slung over their shoulders, and one skinny child even wore a saucepan on his head for a helmet.

'Where did you find that?' Dora wanted to know.

'On the tip, Miss.'

'I don't know what it was doing there, then. All unwanted pots and pans are supposed to be salvaged for recycling. Your helmet will be part of a Spitfire some day.'

'Yes, Miss, p'raps tomorrow. I'm the leader of this lot and I have to look different. Some day I'll be called up and then I'll have a proper tin hat, like them in the Home Guard.'

Dora smiled. It was good to see the boys playing happily together, under a bright blue sky. She hoped and prayed that the war would be over long before Johnny Barron was called to arms. He was only ten years old now. Surely it must come to an end soon?

As for herself, she would be saying goodbye to the green fields of Bryncollen, at least for a little while. She was returning to Coventry soon, to try to deal with those dratted Oattes people. Her colleagues were staying on in Bryncollen; Tansy because she was newly married, and Dinah because she was too starry-eyed to think of anything other than Emlyn Rees.

★   ★   ★

Tansy's wedding had been small as weddings go, but filled with love and happiness. Dora had snivelled happily along with the rest of the small congregation, while watching Sybil Williams out of one eye while the ceremony was going on. She was weeping softly, but whether from emotion or chagrin, it was impossible to say.

'Let's be charitable,' Dora had told Dinah. 'The old girl is just happy because her son has survived to get married, which is a miracle in itself.'

A small reception had been provided by Peter's parents, although far less lavish than it would have been pre-war.

'She said it's a good thing Lady Mary's parents will have to find the food when Mr Paul gets wed,' Elin whispered in Tansy's ear, 'because our store cupboards are as bare as Old Mother Hubbard's now. Still, I do think it's a bit mean. They've got money. They could have scrounged enough stuff to make a better spread.'

'I hope you're not talking about the Black Market,' Tansy hissed. 'That wouldn't do at all, what with Mr Williams being a magistrate.'

'I was only saying, Miss.'

'Well don't. And I'm Mrs Williams now, remember.'

Mrs Williams. Tansy Williams! Now wasn't that something?

Naturally Nellie Smith had shed a few happy tears as well. 'I'm so pleased for you, love! Imagine you marrying into a lot like this, and your chap a pilot! Your Dad didn't know what to make of it all when I told him. Too bad he couldn't be here on your special day, but you know how it is.'

'I'm glad you were able to come, anyway, Mum,' Tansy said warmly.

'I wouldn't have missed it for the world, even though all them train journeys nearly finished me. It wouldn't be so bad if they kept going once they started, but there always seems to be something wrong on the line.'

'Never mind, Mum, you'll have company on the way back.'

'That's right. I like your Mrs Ramsey. We'll get along like a house on fire. Speaking of houses, where are you going to live while your hubby is away fighting the war? Staying on with that old witch of a landlady, are you, or moving into this place with your in-laws?'

'That would be having to choose between the devil and the deep blue sea, Mum,' Tansy had whispered, making sure Sybil wasn't within ear-shot. 'They've given us a cottage on the estate. The man who had it has been called up, and his wife is going back to her family for the duration. It's a bit primitive, but I daresay I can tart it up a bit.'

'My, you've fallen on your feet and no mistake. When I think of us, having to live in digs since the bombing, with six of us, all crammed into three small rooms.'

'Oh, Mum! You'd be welcome to come here. I'd welcome the company, with Peter away.'

'That's a right kind offer, love, but who's to look after your Dad if I'm not there? He couldn't boil an egg to save his life. No, when he gets off work he has to have his fry-ups, and I know what he likes, even if we've had to cut back with everything on the ration.'

'Give him my love, won't you? I wish I could send him a bit of wedding cake, but you know it was only a jam sponge, with no icing. We couldn't get the fruit for a real cake, and of course there wouldn't have been time to make one and let it ripen properly.'

'Never mind, I'll make you a three-tier cake after the war, and we'll eat it all in one sitting, ornaments and all!'

'I'll hold you to that, Mum. Meanwhile, hadn't you better be going? You don't want to miss your train.'

'My goodness, is that the time? Come here, my girl, and give us a kiss. Now then, you be happy, do you hear me?'

Now it had been Tansy's turn to blink away the tears as her mother walked away, without looking back. *Why do we always have to say goodbye to those we love?* She turned to greet her husband as he walked towards her.

'Is your mother off to catch her train? We should be going too, while the light is still good enough to see.'

They were spending their honeymoon in their own little cottage. There wasn't time to go farther afield, for they were to have only one night together before Peter had to report back to camp.

The evening had been too warm to light the fire in the little fireplace but, wrapped in Peter's arms, Tansy looked forward to their future winters together when they would sit here watching the flames leaping up the chimney. She would learn to knit, which would give her something to do while he was away, and after the war, when wool was more readily available again, she would produce all sorts of colourful items. Socks for her husband, and tiny garments for the children they would have.

'How are you going to keep yourself

amused while I'm gone?' Peter had asked, as if reading her mind.

'I don't suppose I'll have much spare time, now I'm a housewife. I'm glad I'm being allowed to stay on at the school, though. That's one good thing about this rotten war, women are encouraged to work outside the home. Dora had to resign when she got married; something about teaching and housewifery not mixing. I suppose I'll be made to stop once the war is over, and things start getting back to normal, but by then we may have children, I expect, so I'd be at home in any case.'

'I suppose you know that my mother would prefer you to stay home from now on? She thinks you should hand in your resignation now, so the governors could find a replacement for the autumn term.'

Tansy managed to bite back a rude comment. However, the expression on her face had said it all, and Peter laughed.

'It's just that she's a bit old-fashioned. Responsible men work to support their wives, not the other way around, and the Williamses do have a position to keep up.'

'I can't see myself trotting around Bryncollen playing Lady Bountiful, Peter. Besides, I'm only the English evacuee. If I tried any of that they'd tell me to go back where I came from. It's just as well I don't speak Welsh; I wouldn't know what they were saying about me.'

'You could meet Mother halfway, though; serve on one or two of her committees, for instance,' Peter had suggested.

'If she invites me, I shall. Otherwise I shan't push my way in.'

'Of course. Listen, Tansy, don't worry about Mother too much. She can be a bit overbearing, I know, but she has a good heart. And when the first grandchild comes along you'll find that you can do no wrong. And don't forget that Paul is getting married in a couple of months. Lady Mary will be coming to live at the house, and she'll be a nice friend for you.'

Tansy had smiled to herself, then. Think of that! Plain Ann Smith, from the back streets of Coventry, hob-nobbing with the aristocracy. She could just imagine herself speaking to her sisters, saying, 'My friend, Lady Mary.' They would give her short shrift if she tried anything like that! She might have married into the gentry, but she was still their little sister, who had to be kept in her place.

'I brought my gramophone across yesterday,' Peter said. 'Shall I put a record on? What would you like, something lively, or something slower? If you like I can roll back the carpet and we can dance.'

And so they had danced on their wedding night to the well-known voice of Vera Lynn reminding them of the days yet to come, 'tomorrow, when the world is free.'

Dora was grateful for Nellie Smith's company on the train. The little woman's stream of cheerful chatter helped to pass the time, and it stopped Dora from brooding. She learned a lot about her young colleague, for Nellie was a very proud mother.

'All the kids left school at fourteen, 'cos they couldn't wait to get started in work. Of course they didn't earn much to start with, but every little bit helps, doesn't it?'

Dora agreed that it did.

'Our Ann, though, she was different. You do know, don't you, that Ann's her real name? The Lord alone knows where she got the idea of calling herself Tansy! Sounds like a weed to me. Still, she would have it, and we're used to it now, apart from her dad, that is. 'Ann she was born and Ann she'll be until the day she dies, as far as I'm concerned.' That's my Bert for you. He speaks as he finds.'

'There's not many children who would stay on at school if they didn't have to,' Dora said. 'They need encouragement to stay on and make something of themselves, as Tansy did.'

'I was willing, but I can't say her dad backed her up. In fact, the day she turned fourteen he heard there was an assistant wanted at Rouse's, the greengrocer's up the road, and he even went in and spoke for it on her behalf. Ann was that cross when she found out, and he was the same when she cheeked him and said she'd die first. 'That can be arranged,' he shouted. You could hear him bawling all the way up the street. Like two peas in a pod, those two are.

'When they'd both calmed down a bit he asked her what was wrong with working at Rouse's? A nice, clean sort of job, and the Rouses are pleasant people. She could enjoy working there. 'Nothing wrong with it for those who didn't have other plans,' she said, but she was going to be teacher. Well, he was that flummoxed, his jaw almost dropped down to his knees. There's never been a teacher in the family, you see; not before our Ann came along.'

'He must be very proud of her now. She's done well for herself and I know that the children respect her.'

'I don't know about that, Mrs Ramsey. He's set in his ways, is Bert, and he's got hold of the idea that she's too big for her boots, if you know what I mean. And marrying this Williams chap hasn't helped. Bert could have got time off work to come to the wedding, but I reckon he was scared of how he'd show himself up against Peter's family. 'I shouldn't know what to say to them. How will I know which fork to use?' I did my best to talk him round, Mrs Ramsey, but it was no use. Once his mind's made up he's like the Rock of Gibraltar.'

Dora smiled ruefully. 'That's a man for you. My Jim can be awkward, too, at times.'

Nellie frowned. 'Lor! Here I am, prattling on, never giving you a chance to get a word in edgewise. What's all this about you coming back to Coventry to sort something out? Ann told me a bit about it but I didn't quite take in what it was all about.'

Dora did her best to put Nellie in the picture. 'I know it all sounds farfetched, but when the girl showed me that snap I couldn't see any way around it. Jim's brother died before I came on the scene, you see, so until now I never knew what he looked like. Jim's mother wasn't one for having studio photographs taken, and back then none of us had cameras.'

'I don't see what you're worrying about, Mrs Ramsey. You know it's nothing to do with your man, so you owe this girl nothing. Paisley! What a name! Whatever happened to the good plain Janes and Lizzies? And if your brother-in-law did father the girl, which we don't know if it's true or not, the poor chap's not here to help her now. Dead and buried. If I were you I'd wash my hands of the lot of them.'

'I only wish I could. I feel I must get to the bottom of this. Even if I never hear from her again I hate the idea of that poor girl believing she has a father who can't be bothered with her.'

'I suppose so.'

'The trouble is, I have no idea where to find these people. Because they were bombed out, they could be anywhere by now. I suppose I'll have to try the WVS or the Salvation Army.'

Nellie pulled at her lip. 'Rose Oattes. I've heard of her. They used to live down our street, and that was the same lot of bombs that destroyed our house as well. I don't know where they've gone now, but I can easily find out for you. The funny thing is, they can't be as badly off as the girl makes out. Rose's husband has a good job at one of the factories and with all the overtime they get, he must have plenty in his pocket.'

'A husband! Are you sure? The girl didn't say anything about him. In fact, according to her the reason she came to see me was because she and her mother were left destitute when the laundry where they worked was also destroyed.'

'Laundry, my foot! That girl works at the Cadena Cafe, and the mother's a housewife. She doesn't go out to business at all. That girl is trying to pull a fast one, Mrs Ramsey, and you mustn't let her get away with it. As soon as we get into Coventry you must call on the police and put them in the picture.'

Dora shook her head. 'Oh, no! I've come this far and I'll see it through. After all, it's my word against Paisley's. She only has to widen her baby-blue eyes and deny everything, and that will be the last of it. The police will give it up as a bad job. No, I'm going to confront her and see what she's got to say from herself. And if I don't worm an apology out of her, I'll eat my hat!'

'Well, it's no good you going round there tonight, not if you want to speak to the husband. Venables, his name is, and he's on the night shift. You'll have to wait till morning. I feel that bad I can't offer you a bed for the night, but as you know we're all of a muddle ourselves.'

'That's quite all right, Mrs Smith. Mr Pepper's niece will put me up. Well, what a good thing it is that you've been able to set me straight. I can't tell you how much I appreciate that.'

'Good luck to you, Mrs Ramsey, and tell our Ann to write and let me how you got on.'

The train began to slow down then, and they both stood up to retrieve their bags from the overhead shelf.

★　★　★

'Mr Venables?'

After a fitful night's sleep, Dora had risen early and had made her way to the place where Rose Oattes was now living. It was a flat on the top floor of a tenement building, and she was surprised that the family had managed to relocate themselves so easily, considering the fact that so many had been made homeless by the bombing. Possibly the man could afford to pay over the odds for accommodation.

'Who wants to know?'

The man on the doorstep was wearing a singlet and a filthy pair of trousers, with a jagged tear at the knee.

'I'd like to see your wife, please. No, don't shut the door. I've come a long way, and I'm not leaving until I speak to her.'

'She ain't up yet. Come back later.'

Dora had dealt with people like him before, although they were usually under the age of eleven! She drew herself up to her her full five-feet-seven-inches. 'Mr Venables, I have something to say that I know you won't want the neighbours to hear.' She nodded in the direction of an elderly woman who had come out to whiten her doorstep.

'Best come in, then.'

She was shown into an untidy kitchen, where the remains of a meal sat on the small wooden table. She plunged right into her story, holding nothing back. 'Well?' she demanded at last. 'What do you say to that?'

While she had been talking his wife had come downstairs and had stood in the doorway, taking all in.

'I'll kill that little devil!' she burst out. 'I've done my best to bring her up right and see how she repays me! And I married Bill here when she was two years old, and he's always treated her fair. She's wanted for nothing all her days.'

'Please excuse me for asking, Mrs Venables, but is it true that Jack Ramsey was her father?'

'Yes, it's true, and Bill here knows all about it. Just two kids, we were really. I was sorry for Jack when he came back from France, and I wanted to give him a bit of comfort. Only once, it took, and there I was, up the spout. Oh, he offered to marry me, but our mam talked me out of it. He wouldn't be able to support me, not in his condition, and he couldn't last much longer anyway. She said the kid would be better off

306

growing up thinking she was her mother, so that's what we did.'

'That part of the story was true, then.'

'Yes, but I didn't know about this scam of hers, I swear. Years ago I told her who her real dad was and I thought that was the end of that. I showed her that snap, of course; it was in a pile of old things I kept in a biscuit tin. She must have found out somehow that he had a brother living locally, and decided to pin it on him.' She gave Dora a fretful look. 'Look, can I beg you not to go to the police? Not for her sake, but ours. We're respectable people, Bill and me.'

'I'll have the hide off that little madam!' Bill Venables growled.

Dora should have implored him to go easy on the girl, but she nodded and held her peace; the little wretch deserved all that was coming to her.

As for Dora, she returned to Wales with a lighter heart.

18

The matrons of Bryncollen had become used to seeing Dinah and Emlyn walking out together, or standing in the queue at the cinema. His mother and aunt were already making plans for the wedding reception, although as yet nothing was settled between the young couple.

'For we cannot expect poor Mrs Blake to manage to put on a 'do' in Coventry,' Gwladys said, although the people of that city would have bridled at such a thought. Despite the fact that many of their streets lay in ruins they were carrying on in splendid fashion, eager to show that they could 'take it' and that Hitler had no chance against such a spirit. Let him do his worst, they felt; the British would come out on top.

'And easier for her to come here for the wedding,' Bron agreed, 'than for half of Bryncollen to go to England.'

'The only fly in the ointment now is your Emo,' Gwladys said. 'Can't you give him a bit of a shove, merch? Dinah is a nice little thing. If he doesn't make his move soon she'll be snapped up by somebody else. Look what happened to that Miss Smith. Married now, and settling down in Bryncollen for good.'

'Na, na. I won't interfere. I've given him hints, mind you, but he only laughs and tells me 'all in good time, Mam!' which I take to mean he's trying to work up to saying something to the girl.'

'Then it's up to me to oil the machinery, so to speak.'

'Just watch out you don't put a spanner in the works, see. I know you, Gwlad Richards! Be careful you don't go too far, and put him off.'

'If he can be put off by a few kind words from his old auntie, then Dinah isn't the girl for him. Don't worry, I'll be subtle.'

* * *

'I want a word with you, Emlyn Rees, boyo!' All her good intentions flew out the window when another week had gone by without the news Gwladys was hoping for.

'What's that about, then, Auntie?'

'You and my lodger, that's what. People are talking, boyo.'

'We've done nothing to be ashamed of, Auntie Gwlad,' Emo said, looking quite affronted.

'That's not what I mean. How long do you intend to keep the poor girl waiting before you make an honest woman of her?'

'None of your business!' he roared. The door slammed behind him. Gwladys stared. He had never been rude to her like that before.

'Was that Emo?' Dinah came into the kitchen, putting her coat on as she came. 'I thought we were going out this afternoon.'

'I think I put my foot in it,' Gwladys told her. 'Go after him, there's a good girl. You should be able to catch him up if you run.'

Looking puzzled, Dinah did as she was told. She found him at the end of the street, looking at the line of hills in the distance.

'Why did you run off like that?'

'Oh, just something Auntie Gwlad said.'

Something about the set of his shoulders told Dinah that it was best not to pry. 'I had a letter from Mum this morning.'

'Oh, aye? What's the news?'

'Joyce is back home. All is forgiven and forgotten, apparently. She's even been given her old job back.'

'What about the husband, then?'

'Better off without him. Mum wonders if he has another wife hidden away somewhere. She says it seems unusual for a man to wait until the age of forty-five to marry for the first time.'

'A man needs to be certain that he's met the right one.'

'And this chap waited for all those years and then picked on Joyce after knowing her for just a few days?'

'Perhaps he did have a previous wife, who died, maybe in the blitz.'

'I wish you wouldn't defend the man, Emo. He lied to Joyce about his prospects. That's not the way a decent man behaves.'

'I was only saying, like!'

'Really, Emo, I don't know what's the matter with you today. I'm going for a walk by myself, and I'll see you later!' She marched off down the street, leaving Emo staring gloomily after her.

* * *

'You're back early, boyo! I thought were going out with Dinah.'

'Now don't you start on at me too, Mam!' Emo said defensively.

'Ah, I see. It was our Gwlad, wasn't it? I told her to keep her ideas to herself. Well, I'm with you, son. That Dinah Blake is not the wife for you, see, and I'm thankful you've seen the light.'

'What? I thought you liked Dinah.'

'Oh, I like her, boyo, but wanting you

to bring her into this house as a daughter-in-law, that's not the same thing, is it?'

'What's wrong with her, then?' Emo was getting riled.

'Nothing at all, for some other man. Now, I've got to get on. I promised myself I'd turn out the front parlour today, and you're holding me back.'

'Mam! You can't leave it like that. Tell me why you think she won't do.'

'Well, since you ask, boyo; for one thing she's English, and for another she's a school teacher.'

He laughed. 'The Welsh stopped fighting the English centuries ago, and as for the teaching, she'll have to give that up when she marries.'

'Look here, Emo. She's used to the city where they have the big shops and art galleries and all the rest. What is there here for her but endless country-side and people who won't make the effort to speak her language? And being a teacher she'll have opinions of her own. She's used to being in charge.

What you need is a nice young girl who will let you be the master in your own home, see.'

With a flick of her duster in his direction, she left him to think about what she had said.

'Forgive me, Lord,' she murmured to herself once he was out of earshot. 'You know I didn't mean those things, but it wasn't a sin to say them, was it, if it brings him to his senses?'

★   ★   ★

On a warm night in June, Emlyn Rees led Dinah Blake into his mother's garden, and proposed marriage. The scent of roses was heavy in the air, for although Bronwen Rees had sacrificed her lawn in order to grow more vegetables, as the government had told everyone to do, she had retained a few of her precious flowers.

'I hope you'll do me the honour of agreeing to be my wife,' he said. His collar suddenly felt tight, and he tugged at it with a shaking finger. He hated wearing a tie, but it had seemed appropriate on this occasion.

'Oh, Emo!' Dinah's eyes were shining like stars. 'Of course I will!'

He swept her into his arms for a kiss that seemed to go on forever.

Glancing out of the kitchen window, Bron hugged herself with delight. 'He's done it, Puss!' she squealed, as the cat rubbed itself against her legs. 'And by the look of it she's said yes! Oh, I knew it would all come right in the end!'

Like lovers everywhere since the beginning of time, Emo and his bride-to-be had a great deal to say to each other. They had so many hopes and dreams, so many plans to make. The years might bring sorrows to them as well as joy, for that is what life is all about. But where there is love there is also strength, and troubles can be surmounted if that love is strong enough.

'I'll love you until the day I die, cariad,' Emlyn whispered. 'I'll never let you down. You can be sure of that.'

Dinah felt as though her heart would burst. 'I love you, too,' she sighed, and when a thrush began to sing in the tree above them she knew that the bird understood what she was feeling, for even wild creatures go about in pairs, and some mate for life, too.

At that moment the war seemed far away and it was as if all the suffering, the privations, and the fears did not exist.

Whatever the future held, they would face it together.

THE END

TAKE A CHANCE ON ME

Teresa Ashby

A marathon brings doctors Anna Curtis and Riordan 'Mac' McKenna together. Anna has moved into the area with her late sister's little boy, Cameron, and Mac offers her a job at his surgery. They become close and Anna falls pregnant. However, when Mac's ex-wife informs her that he doesn't want children, she decides she must move away. Can Mac finally convince her that he loves her, Cameron and the baby?

LOVE IS ALL AROUND

Beth James

When Holly and Granny Jean embark on a round-Britain cruise, Holly little expects to meet up with Ben. Accompanying his grandad, he's wildly attractive, but annoyingly confident. However, after a bad start, Holly is drawn, irresistibly, to a more likeable side to Ben. But Grandad is grumpy, whilst Granny Jean is determinedly cheerful — and the entertainment hostess is more than a little interested in Ben. Holly is left wondering if this is good or bad!

JOURNEY TO PARADISE

Dawn Bridge

Lauren is on holiday in the Bahamas when a tropical storm breaks out. She is left in the care of Glenn, a very attractive American who takes shelter with her. They fall in love — but the problem is, he is the boyfriend of her best friend Anna. Lauren returns home racked with guilt, vowing to forget Glenn, but he has other ideas. Can they find a way of being together without hurting Anna?

THE RIGHT HUSBAND

Kay Gregory

All her life, while Kerry had attracted trouble, Declan was always around to rescue her — an unofficial guardian. She'd almost ended up marrying him. Almost, but not quite. At the eleventh hour her childhood sweetheart turned up to stake his claim to her. After all, Declan's marriage proposal had only been a favour to rescue her from a difficult situation. They weren't really in love . . . Yet jilting Declan at the altar was the hardest thing Kerry had ever done . . .

LOVE IN DISGUISE

Sandra Woolfenden

Everyone loves to read about singer Jasmine James, but often her publicity from the press is untrue. So when she goes away for just one week's holiday in Tunisia, dressed simply and wearing a wig, can she live like other girls her age? But, while she seems to be getting away with it, her falling in love brings complications she hadn't anticipated. Will David understand why she was forced to tell so many lies to cover her tracks?